A Present for Charles Dickens

The children of London

DORÉ

A Present for

for

Charles Dickens

BY
SEON MANLEY

THE WESTMINSTER PRESS
PHILADELPHIA

J Manley

BOOK DESIGN BY DOROTHY ALDEN SMITH

First edition
Published by The Westminster Press®
Philadelphia, Pennsylvania

PRINTED IN THE UNITED STATES OF AMERICA
9 8 7 6 5 4 3 2 1

Library of Congress Cataloging in Publication Data

Manley, Seon.
  A present for Charles Dickens.

SUMMARY: Arriving mysteriously on the Dickens doorstep in a large wicker hamper, the mischievous raven Grip soon establishes himself as close companion to the animal-loving author and tyrant to the rest of the household.
  1. Dickens, Charles, 1812-1870, in fiction, drama, poetry, etc. 2. Ravens—Juvenile fiction. [1. Dickens, Charles, 1812-1970—Fiction. 2. Ravens—Fiction. 3. London (England)—Fiction] I. Title.
PZ7.M3129Pr 1983   [Fic]   82-24862
ISBN 0-664-32706-0

For our grandfather, James J. McLean,
who gave us the gift of Dickens

Contents

(Continued on next page)

1
A Present
for Mr. Charles Dickens

"A PRESENT for Mr. Charles Dickens."

Ella, the parlormaid, looked out the door at the stranger. There was surprise on her face, but there was always surprise on Ella's face because life was so surprising. One never knew who would be outside any door. You never knew whom you were going to entertain. The Dickenses had so many friends. You never knew quite what day it was, and you never knew what kind of a present anybody had for anybody else.

She wondered if she shouldn't send the stranger to the basement entrance. He carried a wicker box that was nearly large enough to hold the holiday turkey that the printers sent the master each year. But no, this man looked very important. No messenger.

"Come in," she said. "I'll call the master."

"No need," he said. "No need." And he vanished down the snow-covered steps.

The snow surprised Ella too, and yet why shouldn't there be snow in December? Why shouldn't the master be getting a gift? It was lighter than any turkey should be. Strange. There were all sorts of rustling noises coming from inside the box and a tap, tap, tap. A tap, tap, tap. Why, it sounded like the devil himself. And that strange noise: caw, caw, caw.

She dropped the box in surprise, and then, as Ella often did, she screamed, which also surprised her. Transfixed, she looked at the box and saw the top move. She screamed again. The top snapped back (she never would forget it; it was a mystery, it was; she never would forget it in all her life). First, out came a long black beak, sharp as a pencil, it was, and two glary eyes looking at her. Then the rest of the very strange bird emerged.

Ella sized it up cautiously. It was long. It seemed nearly two feet long. Maybe longer. The longest, tallest bird she had ever seen in the world, and the meanest. It flew back to the top of the basket with a fine brisk motion, smashed the top down again, and then sat there as if for all the world defying Ella to scream again. And just because she would not be done in by any bird, she did—she screamed again.

The bird looked at her in utter disgust, and when young Charley, not quite three, came toppling down the stairs as though he had just been spun loose from a nest, and the master himself—Ella was still screaming.

"A birdie," said young Charley.

"What have we here?" said Mr. Dickens. "You sounded like Bill Sikes himself were after you, Ella."

"A bird, sir," she said. "Somebody sent you a bird."

"A bird indeed," said Dickens.

"A strange bird," she said. "The devil himself, he is. Why, look at him. He's looking at you right now."

"Why, so he is," said the master. "So he is. A grand bird. It's a raven, Charley. I've never seen a raven so close up." And he went to stretch out his hand to the bird.

"He's got a grip on that basket, sir."

"So he does. He doesn't seem to want to make friends with me yet, does he?"

"He's the devil himself," said Ella.

"Come here, birdie," said Charley. Then the bird looked at young Charley with caution. He flew up to the rung of a chair, all the time saying something like, "Hello, hello, hello, bowwow, bowwow. What's the matter here? Hello."

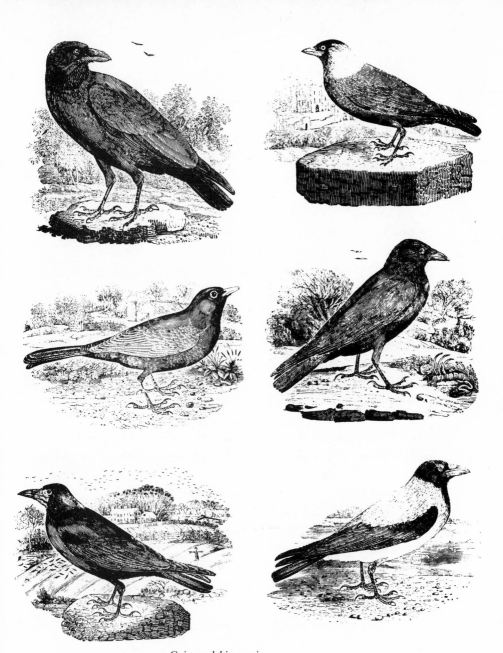

Grip and his cousins

The Raven	The Jack-Daw
The Blackbird	The Magpie
The Rook	The Hooded Crow

ARTIST UNKNOWN

He did have a sort of supernatural look about him. The devil himself as Ella would say.

The bird looked at the three onlookers. They looked at him. Dickens once more stretched out his arm, and the bird moved politely away. He listened to them jabbering together, the bird did, with very polite attention, and it was obvious that he understood every word that was said. He turned his head from one to the other as if he sat in judgment. He would not lose a word.

"Look at him," said Dickens. "Was there ever such a knowing imp as that?"

The raven knew just what he meant. He put his head to one side, and his bright eyes studied his surroundings. He wondered if he should take up with this strange new family or not, and then he gave an answer. An answer in a strange supernatural voice that set up Ella's screaming all over again. A voice harsh and distant. It seemed to come from all of his feathers rather than from out of his mouth. And the voice seemed to say, "Hello, hello, hello. Keep up your spirits. Never say die. Bowwow, bowwow, bowwow. I'm a devil, I'm a devil, I'm a devil. Hurray." And then he let out a strange whistle.

"What? What? What?" said young Charley excitedly.

"Listen," said Dickens.

"I can just tell that he knows what I'm saying. Talk, birdie," said Charley.

"Go away," said Ella.

And the bird suddenly flapped his wings as if he were bursting with laughter.

Charley was delighted. He clapped his hands.

"A friend," said Charley.

"A very good friend, indeed," said Mr. Dickens.

"Shall I get somebody to catch him?" said Ella.

"Catch him? Indeed, he's not going anywhere," said Dickens.

"You're not keeping him, sir?" she said.

"Keeping him? Why, my dear Ella, I do believe he's the one that's decided to keep us."

"He's got a terrible grip. He'll scratch the chairs," said Ella.

"And that, my dear Ella, is what we will call him. Grip, the raven," said Dickens.

He turned to go up the stairs, followed by young Charley, and right behind them, as though he were learning to walk into a new home, Grip followed majestically. The bird hopped carefully from step to step.

Downstairs at the door, Ella looked up. Mysteries, she thought, surprises. The world was all a surprise, it was.

But mark her words. That bird was a devil!

2
No. 1 Devonshire Terrace

"HERE COMES that Dickens bird. Isn't he an imp?" said the old crossing sweeper, Billy, to the woman who pressed a coin into his hand. "Remarkable bird, that. Getting a reputation around here. Just like," said the old man, holding a finger to his nose and winking an eye, "just like Mr. Dickens himself. A couple of wonders they are!"

"You are quite right," said the woman. She happened to be Jane Carlyle, the wife of Thomas Carlyle. The very night before they had met young Dickens at a party. She had, indeed, noticed how the young man did strut. Well, he had a right to, and besides he was a joyous companion. She had left her card at his new home so that the budding friendship would flower.

Grip and the Dickens family and the servants were all new tenants of the handsome house, No. 1 Devonshire Terrace, just south of Regent's Park in London. Charles Dickens was twenty-seven years old. *Oliver Twist* had made him a celebrity.

His family had grown along with his other accomplishments. He and his wife, Catherine, known as Kate, were the proud parents of Charley. This "Living Wonder," as Dickens had further christened him, had been joined by a baby sister Mamie. And now, at the time of the move to Devonshire Terrace, there was a demanding young infant named Katie in the cradle.

A new queen, Victoria, was on the throne; a new writer, Charles Dickens, was in the news. He intended to keep it that

6

way. He wanted a rich man's house, a houseful of friends, and yes, pets. Frankly, he was uncomfortable about his shabby childhood.

He kept quiet about the embarrassing fact that his grandmother had been a housemaid, his grandfather a butler. He hid the facts of his father's imprisonment for debt; he hid his own "horrible nightmare" of childhood, when he had been put to work at a blacking factory as a very young boy.

But he could not and, indeed, had no desire to hide his genius. All London today was talking about him. Dickens (who often called himself the Inimitable) took almost childish delight in his new house. He examined every nook and cranny with the help of two equally curious companions.

Charles Dickens at the time of Grip's arrival

MACLISE

"See," said young Charley, at every new discovery.

"Caw," summoned Grip, as he hid behind every curtain.

The entrance to the house, 1 Devonshire Terrace, lay back a little from the street. It had a majestic portico of brick and stone. One went in the door to warmth and happiness. A large vestibule, a great square hall, a stairway curving up to the left. It was on the right, however, in the library, with steps descending into the garden, that Dickens and Grip found their greatest satisfactions. Not that Grip wasn't happy everywhere. Happy in the dining room with the ornamental columns, happy in the garden, happy in the coach house, where he soon learned to sleep on the back of one of the horses.

Of course, Grip was not universally liked. Mrs. Dickens had greeted him with, "Absolutely not, Charles."

Charles Dickens had answered back, "Absolutely, Kate."

The raven arrived at a time of renewal. He tried to hang on the great mahogany doors as they were rehung. He jumped from the discarded wooden mantels onto the carved marble such as often dignified the houses of London's great writers.

The old Dickens home on Doughty Street had contained only ordinary, often used furniture. But for this house, for this grand house, everything new was needed. Curtains festooned all the rooms, rich in colors, heaped with pockets and creases—great hiding places not only for Grip but for all the treasures that he soon fastened upon.

The carpets were deep-piled as a soft field in any meadow, and the shining mirrors reflected the lights on the nights when Dickens entertained. Soon the rooms were festooned with holly and boxwood, with ivy and with mistletoe because Christmas was coming, and Charles Dickens, almost single-handed, was going to bring back the old-fashioned Christmas to the hearts of everyone.

Downstairs, in the great and cavernous kitchen, Grip also made himself at home. He soon realized that area was controlled by a tyrant as tyrannical as Grip himself. The tyrant, of course, was Cook, a Victorian mistress of the nether regions, an individual of strength and genius, a woman who commanded pots and pans and stoves and scullery maids, a woman who commanded respect.

Their introduction had been dramatic.

"Well now, bird," said Cook, with her hands on her hips. "We shall see what we shall see." She stared hypnotically at the bird, who almost put his wings on his hips and stared back. "I don't have all day to be staring at you," said Cook. But the bird never made a move. "I don't have all day to look at a devil like you." And she would turn her back, only to have Grip caw, "More, more, more," and pick up a currant from the great pudding that was in preparation, and fly away.

"A devil of a bird," Cook said, as she would call out her ingredients to the kitchen. "Now get me those currants that you cleaned, Bess. Chop that pound of beef suet. Stone the raisins. Gather the apples and chop them." Then as the coachman came in, "I need everybody's help today. Come, Topping," she said to the coachman. "Beat that old spice very fine. Sugar it to your taste. Now brandy and wine. Altogether. Altogether. This is going to be one of the best of all mince pies."

"You make a fine pie, Cook," said Topping.

"I'm Cornish, that's the reason," she said.

"Finest of all. How many will you make?"

"As many as that bird won't steal me out of. Him with his taste of currants and his pleasure in raisins. And as many houses as you can eat mince pies in during Christmas, Topping, as many happy months will you have in the ensuing year."

And as though to crown those wise words, Grip would flutter in, stand on the back of the chair, and place an order, or so it sounded.

Cook soon began to think that she could hear him speak. He came with a message, certainly. The master wanted his favorite drink. A little sherry, hot water, sugar, nutmeg, and lemon juice. Liked it so much he was always writing about it, they told her. Liked it as much as all the excitement of the twelve days of

Christmas. Nothing but a big boy at times. Look how he took to that bird!

Well, bird or no bird, he was the master, and he should have his Christmas pudding and the greatest of Christmases ever.

Then she turned her back again. That bird, that devil of a bird had stolen a piece of cold roast. She picked up a broom, and Grip made for the library.

This was the first true library that Dickens had had since he was a boy, and that library had been just a cold and miserable attic. But it was in that library that he had befriended his first bird. The imaginary parrot. He would never forget that parrot, nor the book he had found it in, nor that cold and dreary attic. Cold and miserable, but he called it later "that blessed little room." Blessed with the first books he had ever seen, with the stories of Don Quixote, Tom Jones, of the Vicar of Wakefield, and best of all Robinson Crusoe and his parrot. Yes, books were the best friends that any lonely child could have.

He often remembered, too, that terrible, terrible day as his father's fortunes became more and more depleted. Their way of life had become so treacherous that all belongings had to be pawned. It was he, that boy Charles, who had to take those very books to the pawnshop.

Never, never would he forget that, and never, Dickens had sworn, would he be that poor again. Never! And he would leave the library door and revel in the richness of the curtains and the richness of the rugs, delight in the sound of his own carriage at the door, and like his own character Oliver Twist, know that in some part of himself he wanted even more.

Then he would laugh because there would be Grip on the floor, jumping up and down, reflecting his master's very desires, and saying quite intelligently, "More, more. I'm a devil. I'm a devil. More, more."

3
Ella's Enemy

MORE. Why, that was the very word to describe Christmas, Ella mumbled to herself.

More work. That's what. More guests for Mr. Dickens! More holly dropping more berries. More.

And what was this? A feather. From that devil of a raven.

Who would have ever believed a good parlormaid such as herself would be cleaning up after a raven? If the devil wore feathers, he would look as wicked as Grip.

Ella threw it into the fireplace; it caught fire, sputtered, and released the stench of burnt feathers. She had a good mind to give notice. They could choose. Ella or that bird.

Maybe, though, that wasn't such a good idea. The master was thoroughly entranced with that bird. It hypnotized him, that bird did.

She was startled when the doorbell rang.

The master at the doorway, and that—that bird on his shoulder.

"Good morning, Ella. The mistress up? No, I suppose not. What, even the Living Wonder still abed? What shall we do with them, Grip? Here we've been scrambling through the snow-covered streets. Up and away through Regent's Park, the wind howling; the trees bowing and bending to the wind, lest it should do them harm. Cowards, those trees, eh, Grip? Look at him, Ella. Did you ever see a finer bird?"

"No, sir," said Ella, taking Dickens' greatcoat.

"Brave Grip, Ella. Nothing worries him. When the wind rolls him over in the snow, he turns manfully to bite it. Show Ella, Grip."

And Grip, like a tumbling acrobat, flipped a somersault on the floor.

Ella watched as though she had been commanded to cheer the devil's imp himself. Words of praise, however, would not come for the demon, no matter how she struggled for them.

"See how fierce he looks? Grip, good Grip has quarreled with every snow shape on the ground, every twig. He's been worrying the shadows in the street like a bulldog."

While Ella was so stupefied by this performance of Dickens and the bird, Grip was exhilarated. Hearing the frequent motion of his name in a tone of exultation, Dickens said later to his friends, always made Grip crow like a cock.

The crowing made Ella tremble. But the bird had not finished.

He began to run over his various phrases of speeches with such rapidity, thought Dickens admiringly, and in so many varieties of hoarseness, that they sounded like the murmurs of a crowd of people.

Ella could take no more. She covered her ears and bolted to the cozy world belowstairs. A cup of tea was what she needed to settle her nerves.

But as she reached the last step to the kitchen, she saw the bird hopping down the very same step.

They entered the kitchen together.

Ella was sure that bird was her enemy.

Grip stared at Ella. He seemed to know he terrified her.

"Don't look at him that way, Ella!" said Cook. "Don't look stupid. That bird just seems to be encouraged in his deviltry if you make him feel superior."

Although, thought Cook to herself, it was perfectly obvious that Grip seemed to have more wit than Ella.

"I'll just turn my back to him," said Ella. "I'll just sit here and help you stone the fruit. It's just that he seems like some supernatural agent, he does."

Ella seated herself sedately and reached for the tin basin of fruit.

Suddenly, out of nowhere, Ella swore later, Grip landed on her shoulder and cried with a hoarse voice in her ear,

"Halloa! Halloa, halloa, halloa! Bowwow-wow. What's the matter here? Halloa!"

Ella screamed. She flung out her arms, knocking over tins of flour and sugar, scattering currants and plums to the floor.

"Ella," screamed Cook. The red and green holiday ribbons in her cap streamed out in fury. (Mr. Dickens always complimented her on her ribbons.)

But no scream of Cook's could outdo Ella's. Ella's scream brought Topping and the very young Scottish stableboy, Jemmy.

"What's the matter with her?" said Jemmy, fascinated by Ella's performance.

Her scream had shattered into tears. Now she cried violently, clutching both hands over her heart, as if to keep it from splitting into small fragments.

Everyone was so engrossed with Ella's range of sobs that they did not see the master himself enter the kitchen.

Ella looked up and saw Dickens staring at her.

Her sobs changed into a groan and then a cough.

"He's wrung my heart, sir," she said.

"And who, Ella, is he, if I may ask? That one?" asked Dickens, gesturing to Jemmy, whose face flushed.

"No, sir."

"Our noble Topping?" said Dickens.

"No, sir. The bird, sir. Grip. He's like a vulture, sir."

"A different bird altogether," said Dickens amused. "Say you're sorry, Grip. Say you're sorry to Ella."

"Look at him," said Cook. "Did you ever see such an imp?"

Grip looked at the disaster he had caused. He studied the floor with the trampled fruit and appeared to make a note to himself as to what would be the tastiest.

Dickens summoned him to attention, however, with one cry. "Grip!"

Grip put his head on one side, his bright eye shining like a diamond. He was painfully silent. Then, in that supernatural voice that so terrified Ella, he answered Dickens. The bird's voice seemed to come through his thick feathers rather than out of his mouth. "Halloa, halloa, halloa."

The bird paused for effect. As an actor he could compete with Ella anytime.

Then when he had caught everybody's attention, he balanced himself perfectly on tiptoe. He proceeded to move his body up and down, in what Dickens later described as sort of a grave dance.

He accompanied the movements with his own libretto. "I'm a devil, I'm a devil."

His audience stood around him; each with his or her own personal reaction.

Cook was delighted with his spunk. Grip was an imp but a delightful one. And he knew what she felt. There would be no fooling that bird.

Ella thought of screaming again, but saw she had lost center stage and settled for a few tears.

Topping, the groom, simply said, "Call him, Jemmy. Get back to the stable."

But Jemmy, who had been awakened during the night by the fact that Grip had insisted on keeping awake one of the horses in the stable, just muttered. "Call him! But who can make Grip come? I don't think he slept at all in the stable. Nor the horses either. I went in during the night and saw those two eyes shining like two sparks. He was talking to himself, cawing away."

"Come, Grip," said Dickens.

The bird looked at him, swelling his wings against his side as if he were bursting with laughter.

He zoomed to the floor, rescued a Christmas currant, and when he had savored it like a corvine gourmet, landed on Dickens' shoulder.

"You're a natural character, Grip. I'll make you famous."

And bird and writer went upstairs.

4
"A Clever Corbie, Indeed!"

IT WAS only two days short of Christmas, and Grip seemed to have all the usual anxiety of a very young child. Nothing that he did was right. He was underfoot, overhead; he sat in the wrong chairs; he had disturbed the horses in the stable.

That was not all. Grip had acquired a habit that was not to make him dearly beloved by the women. He nipped ankles. Perhaps it was a sign of affection, but it was an affection that was not returned. In those days when the women wore dresses almost like sails, so that a slight wind might almost topple them, this attack upon their dignity and their ankles at the same time was more than they could bear.

Mrs. Dickens did not find the raven amusing during the pressure of the holidays. The children had cried the night before when Grip had tried to elicit a little interest from them. And even at one of the constant dinner parties, which Dickens had given in this new house to celebrate his new respectability as the master of a fine home, Grip cawed so wildly that he defeated some of the finest conversationalists in London.

The Irish artist Daniel Maclise, who had dined with Dickens the night before, had called him: "A clever corbie, indeed!"

As soon as Maclise had said the very word "corbie," Grip came to attention, as though he actually knew the old Celtic name for raven.

Grip fanned his large throat hackles at the same time as he stretched his head and neck forward.

"A portrait, a portrait, I must do a portrait of him," said Maclise.

"And I shall do a poem about him," said Dickens' friend, the novelist William Ainsworth, who admired, he said, Grip's solemn tone.

But in the midst of the conversation, Grip had tried to steal a bit of baba au rhum. He had been rapidly dispatched from the room.

Grip was indeed in difficulty. Topping and Jemmy had tossed him from the stables and locked the door upon him, even when he cawed at the door. The mistress had secured all doors upstairs, and Cook had barricaded herself in the last-minute flurry of the true artist in preparations for the Christmas dinner. The children were tired and cranky with too much excitement.

Dickens himself was exhausted. He never knew quite what his feelings were about Christmas. They were so, well, overwhelming, that he could not separate them. But he knew he had to have a little peace. He had retreated to his library. He looked out into the garden that stretched in the back of Devonshire Terrace.

There was Grip looking at him through the window. What a curiously alive bird he looked. Wasn't it in the old Norse legends that he had read as a child about those two ravens who had sat on the shoulders of Odin the god and, knowing everything, told him everything?

Dickens went to the door, almost as a boy would, tiptoeing half bent so no one would hear him, and let the mischief-maker in.

Then Dickens sat down and studied his new pet for a long time.

First, he studied Grip's walk. Yes, he did strut, but at other times he had a particular hop that reflected joy, and still other times a very sedate walk. But most often, Dickens noted, Grip neither walked nor ran, but had a strange pace of his own. Like what?

Ah, thought Dickens, I know that walk. The walk of a very particular gentlemen with exceedingly tight boots on, trying to walk fast over loose pebbles. "Come here, Grip."

The bird came to his hand. Dickens could understand how he might (and did) startle some people. Of majestic length, he was a fine example of a raven. His wings had been clipped, of course, as was the custom of the day, so that he could not fly far. And Dickens hoped that the custom of keeping any wild bird would vanish. But Grip had grown accustomed to people, indeed he enjoyed people.

In appearance, Grip was nearly all black, but when Dickens took him to the window, in the right light, his plumage took on a strange iridescence.

There, something had startled Grip.

"You're both rascals," said Dickens as he looked out the window and saw a rook, a cousin of the raven, stealing some berries from the ivy outside the window.

"You'd both steal anything," said Dickens.

Grip made no answer. Instead his throat feathers seemed to sprout, and the feathers over his eyes gave him an unusual appearance of alertness, intelligence—and rascality.

5
The Holly
and the Ivy

DICKENS had been awakened early Christmas morning by the sound of carolers. He had dressed rapidly. Time enough later for the clothes of the dandy that he had grown to love so much. Throwing on whatever was at hand, he went out into the wide garden beyond his home. There he saw the old gardener humming to himself and called out, "Merry Christmas. What are you humming, Patterson?"

"Oh," he said, "I'm singing to the holly."

"To the holly?"

"Yes, sir. To the holly and to the ivy. That's how we old gardeners celebrate this season. You hang them in the house, and we sing to them out here."

"Let me hear," said Dickens.

"Oh, I've got no voice, sir. But you got to sing to the Christmas greens, you know. A voice doesn't matter to them. Well, if you like, here it is, sir. Forgive my voice. This one's called 'Holly':

> "Here comes Holly that is so gent,
> to please all men, is his intent,
> Alleluia!

> "Whosoever against holly do cry,
> in a rope shall be hung full high,
> Alleluia!"

Choosing Christmas mistletoe

PHIZ

"Fascinating," said Dickens, a smile beaming across his face. His scarf bobbed in the cold breeze. "Fascinating."

"Caw," came from beside him. "Caw."

"Oh, it's that bird again, sir. That bird. What a noisy fellow he is. Not like the ivy. Ivy's got a song too, sir. Would you like to hear it?"

"Yes," said Dickens with less enthusiasm.

"Caw," interrupted Grip loudly, and the gardener turned away in disgust.

Grip had the feeling that it was going to be a good day.

Dickens had the feeling that it was going to be a good day.

Oh, how he loved Christmas! Not always with a straight love, because it was so filled with the anguish of the past. But now, like any child, he went to take a look, before his very small children came down, at his favorite of favorites, all the decorations.

"Who wouldn't love Christmas," he shouted to Grip. "It's the happiest time of the year. It is a season of mirth and cold weather. It is a time of mistletoe and red-berried laurel and soups and sliding."

Grip ignored him.

Dickens went in and looked around the room where the Christmas evergreen branches reigned in delight. How beautifully they were hung with toys. Would Christmas become more and more popular now that Queen Victoria was on the throne? Maclise said she didn't have just boughs, but a beautiful Christmas tree that was brilliantly lighted by a multitude of little tapers that everywhere sparkled and glittered with bright objects.

Among the boughs at the Dickens home, however, there was plenty of room for rosy-cheeked dolls hiding behind the green leaves and real watches with movable hands dangling from innumerable twigs.

There was doll furniture among the boughs for Dickens' baby girls—French polished tables, chairs, wardrobes, clocks, and various other articles of domestic furniture wonderfully made

The Dollmakers

PHIZ

of tin at Wolfington's, as if in preparation for some fairy house-keeping.

For Charley there were jolly, broad-faced little men, much more agreeable in appearance than any real men, and no wonder, for their heads too often showed them to be full of sugarplums. There were fiddles and drums; there were tambourines, workboxes, paint boxes, sweetmeat boxes, peep-show boxes, and all kinds of boxes. And best of all, there were books, beautifully packaged, everywhere. What magnificent presents!

Each year, Dickens supposed, presents would change as the children got older. Would the hanging boughs look to his children, as they came down in their nightclothes, as they had looked to him in his childhood? He remembered just how they had looked to him as a child, the toys buried in the evergreens.

Funny how he remembered those toys. They had terrified him. He was trying to be careful with his own children that their toys would never be quite so frightening that they would dream about them. That mechanical frog he had received as a boy, for example; there was no knowing where it wouldn't jump, and when it flew over the candles and came back upon his hand with its spotted back red on a green ground—it was horrible.

Almost to surprise him, Grip flew close and landed on his shoulder.

"Oh, Grip, what a strange day. So filled with past dreams, fears, and pleasure. Why do I look at this Christmas tree and think of all those stories of the Arabian Nights that I read so much when I was young? Why do I think of Robinson Crusoe and his parrot on the desert island, eh, Grip?"

Why did Dickens think of the toy theaters? As a boy he had imagined the ladies in their feathers in their boxes. How could one put together so much excitement with paste and glue and gum and water?

He went to the window, and once more went out into the garden and saw the old gardener and the winter prospect of his great house. But suddenly the past came back to him: the low-lying misty ground, the fens and fogs that one could see in Chatham, his childhood home.

He wondered when the children had gotten to sleep. This was an old house, an old house with ghosts, he thought.

Was it really true, as his old grandmother used to say, that the ghosts returned on Christmas? He remembered the story of the orphan boy in his own family, and, as he stood there, imagining himself lost, wondered about that time when he had had no Christmas at all.

To distract Dickens, Grip began to flutter around the room. Suddenly there was the sound of the young Charley coming down the stairs, and the babies screaming with delight and pleasure as they saw the tapers on the tree.

"Merry Christmas," Dickens cried out.

"Merry Christmas," cried out Charley. "Merry Christmas! Lights! Lights! Christmas lights! Toys! Dolls! Christmas!"

Grip took a look cautiously around the room, did a dance, half flight, half ballet steps, then leaped up to the corner where mistletoe was hanging, stole a berry, flew to the floor, called out, "I'm a devil."

He nipped Charley's ankle. There was a scream followed by laughter, and then Grip's caw, and the words again, "I'm a devil."

Gathering his children up in his arms, Dickens looked at the preening bird on the floor and said, "You are, indeed. Merry Christmas, Grip, though. Merry Christmas!"

6
Christmas Boxes

GRIP glued himself to the top of the highest rung on the old ladder-back chair in the library. He seemed as preoccupied as Dickens himself, who sat at the large library table with its top in fine disarray.

In one corner was a collection of boxes of all sizes, in another were envelopes of different shapes. Scattered about were sheets of wrappers, colorful paper, small sums of money in silver, and even smaller sums in gold.

Immediately in front of Dickens lay a strange assortment of objects, among which were:

1 silver comb decorated with filigree
1 bouquet of colored ribbons
1 top hat (small size)
1 top hat (large size)

Dickens appeared to be studying them carefully. Grip eyed them with the same fascination, particularly the gold sovereign, especially the silver half crowns, but most particularly the silver comb.

"How do you wrap a top hat, Grip? An impossible feat. I know. I know. You have that look on you today that nothing is impossible. What a strange companion you are. Today I would like you to talk, but of course you will not. Yet you chatted through Christmas as though you were Father Christmas' emissary, and, as usual, gave Ella a fearful fright."

"Caw," agreed Grip.

"That's the reason for this comb."

Dickens held it up, and it glistened in the December sunlight that splashed across his desk.

Grip eyed it with approval. "Caw."

"Caw," imitated Dickens. "What sort of conversation is that? Are you feeling sickly? I guess everybody is after Christmas. And now St. Stephen's Day."

In England, over the years, it came to pass that the day after Christmas, St. Stephen's Day, eventually became Boxing Day, when Christmas boxes with small gratuities of money or gifts were presented to the underpaid who performed so many of the duties that made Victorian life not only possible but comfortable.

All expected and received such gifts, and Dickens, who could be extremely generous, took special delight in the custom and in the giving.

"Give me the old-fashioned way, Governor," old Billy, the crossing-sweeper, had said to Dickens that morning. "Give me the frost and a clear sky. Give me the old Christmas. I did uncommon well then. There were good times then. Christmas spirit. Begging your pardon, you being a writer and all. You'd know that—the old-fashioned way."

As he spoke, he was sweeping the snow briskly. His cheeks were apple red; his eyes were as black as Grip's and just as sparkling. He kept shaking his head like a terrier dog, and his old hat was limp from where it was touched day in and day out, as he showed proper respect for his "betters."

"Yes, Governor, the old-fashioned way. That's something to write about. Can't read myself, but I like the pictures, and the theater, sir, and Christmas, sir. Those old Christmases, they were different, sir."

"How?" said Dickens, entranced as always by one of the old characters of London.

"Why? The money, sir."

"The money?"

Boxing Day

CRUIKSHANK

"Yes, sir. The old penny pieces, sir. That was real money, sir. You knew it was money."

Dickens found his face flushed even in the cold. He remembered penny pieces as a boy in the blacking factory when they were all that stood between him and hunger.

"Yes, give me the old penny pieces, sir. Not that I'm not grateful for your box, sir. Very grateful, sir." And he tipped his hat. "But that old money was *heavy*, sir. Real money. It broke your pocket. How's the bird, sir?"

Dickens laughed. "He's beginning to get a reputation in the neighborhood."

"No wonder, sir. One of the finest birds I've ever seen. Walks down here."

"To the square?" asked Dickens, surprised.

"That's right. Walks down, strutting like someone out of the pantomime. And then comical as Punch, sweeps with me. Those wings are like brooms at times. The way that birds uses them! A happy New Year, Governor."

"A very happy New Year, Billy."

"Give that bird a halloa for me and a happy New Year."

"He seems to be in hiding this morning. Made too much of Christmas night."

Indeed, Grip continued silent, except for an expressive caw that could have been, indeed must have been, a case of overindulgence in Cook's Christmas pudding.

Cook had been considerably perturbed when Dickens had left a message to have the dustman sent up to the library, and Ella had commiserated with her.

"It's a mystery," said Ella. "Now the dustman. Bad enough that devil of a bird with the run of the house. But a dustman!"

"Likes characters," said Cook grudgingly and, because she never liked to agree with Ella, muttered darkly. "Even if St. Stephen's Day means that this afternoon is a holiday, up you go, Ella, no slacking off."

"Suppose it will be the chimney sweep, the postman, the butcher, baker, and candlestick-maker next," muttered Cook. "He will have to see them all."

But Dickens simply sent word at the end of the day that he would see only the lamplighter.

Lamplighters had always fascinated Dickens. He felt they were a strange primitive people who rigidly adhered to the old customs and ceremonies that had been handed down to them from father to son.

And what about daughters? Why, every daughter of a lamplighter had talent enough for it and would have been lamplighters themselves except for the prejudices of society.

"Let women have their rights," Dickens was to have one of

his characters say in his humorous tale *The Lamplighter's Story*. But that emancipation hadn't come yet, and didn't then, and consequently they confined themselves to the bosoms of their families, cooked the dinners, mended the clothes, minded the children, comforted their husbands, and attended to the housekeeping generally. "It's a hard thing upon the women, gentlemen, that they are limited to such a sphere of action as this; very hard."

Kate Dickens, although now rewarded with help, still found the running of her household took up her energies. How did Charles find time to write all those books, sometimes walk all night, host many dinner parties every month—always be on the move? Besides the time spent in teaching that bird to talk (although Grip was beginning to endear himself to her). And now that new pony in the stable—ostensibly a gift for young Charley, but another character that entranced Dickens himself.

Kate was absolutely right that the new pony had captured Dickens' imagination. He was late wrapping the gifts for his household.

The first was the silver comb.

Grip watched it with pleasure. All birds are attracted by shining objects.

"Caught your eye, did it, Grip? You are not to harass Ella. Grip, this is by way of a penance for the mischief you give her. And how do you like these?"

Dickens held up the colored ribbons that would go to Cook.

Grip allowed himself a caw.

Dickens modeled the top hat that would go to Topping.

He danced around the room, as limber as a chimney sweep. And like a chimney swift, Grip soared at the color, picked up a colored sheet of paper, and flew out of the room.

"Come back, Grip," Dickens called.

"Talking to a bird as though he was human," Ella scolded under her breath.

"I know where you're going, Grip."

And Dickens was right. He couldn't wrap Topping's top hat, and he *didn't* wrap Jemmy's smaller hat. He wanted to see Jemmy's face when he presented it to him.

Jemmy had been promoted. At thirteen (a small thirteen at that) he had just been made a full undercoachman and the complete master of the irascible pony that Dickens had christened Whisker.

7
Whisker, the Pony

GRIP had managed right from the very beginning to get a grip on the Dickens household. If he had any true devotion, it was to Dickens himself. But he was a marvelously self-contained bird, imperious (for after all wasn't he one of the birds of the gods?), knowing (after all, wasn't he one of the symbols of wisdom?), and as he seemed to feel, preening his own feathers, inimitable.

Charles Dickens thought of himself, particularly in the character of Boz, equally inimitable, referring to himself as such in letters, or even in conversation. Dickens' emotions often wavered from a feeling of almost invincibility to a feeling of acute depression. It all depended on his work. When things went well with his writing, life could not be better. When they went poorly, life was oppressive in every way. He had too many children, too many debts, parents who were still cadging from him, a world that was dark and rarely had sunlight.

Grip, his raven, seemed to be unusually responsive to these moods. Occasionally, the bird even evolved a sort of dance to amuse the writer. And other times he staggered around as though he had sampled more than a little of the superb punch that Dickens personally prepared for his friends.

But now Grip had competition. New competition. And he took to it as those who are inimitable often do: very poorly. It was not two-legged competition; Grip seemed capable of handling any human being that came his way, from Cook to Ella to the very little baby Katie, who used to clap her hands in joy at the sight of the black bird. No, the two-legged people were quite in his control. The four-legged beings in the world of the stable were more likely at the moment to be his nemesis.

The purchase had been made, a magnificent purchase, a purchase that Jemmy approved of very much. Jemmy had supervised the building of a small stable within the stable for Whisker's domain. As Whisker was so singled out, he had not bothered the coach horses, nor had he bothered Grip.

Grip continued to sleep quite comfortably on the backs of the coach horses. He let them share his slumber and his insomnia.

When insomnia bothered him, he pecked at the wooden walls. The stable was in poor shape. "Needs a painting," said Jemmy. "Needs a painting, very badly."

"Needs a painting," said Topping. "But they're putting it all in the house. Don't think of the animals."

"Oh, they think of the animals, the master does. Just haven't gotten around to it," said Jemmy.

But Topping was feeling very grouchy that day.

"Something's got to be done about that Whisker. Indeed, I can't do a thing with that Whisker. He stares me in the eye worse than the raven does. Then he'll look at me and roll his eyes, slobber, he will. If I reach my hand out with a bit of carrot, he's as snappy as a terrier."

The top hat had been the last straw.

It's true that on Boxing Day the master had given the usual gift of money and a new top hat. But the point was, explained Topping patiently, that Topping had been perfectly happy with his old top hat. As a matter of fact, he loved that old top hat. Why, Whisker hadn't been in Topping's presence for more than a few

This pony was part of a private menagerie well known in London

ARTIST UNKNOWN

minutes when he had chewed that hat as though he were part goat.

Jemmy listened to Topping's tirade with a smile he tried to hide. It was true that Whisker had not taken at all to Topping.

Whisker was the most independent pony he had ever seen.

Grip was the most independent bird he had ever seen.

Grip would pace in front of Whisker's stable, but even his most concerted movements would not phase Whisker. The bird simply did not exist, as far as Whisker was concerned. He would continue at his oats as though that was all he had on his mind. That strange, comic black raven could not distract him.

Grip tried further skills. "Bowwow."

These threatening words could not shatter Whisker's composure.

Grip edged nearer to the bag of oats that so held Whisker's interest. He opened his bill—the coach horses were used to Grip's snapping up the spray of fallen oats, but not Whisker.

His hoofs played a wicked tattoo, and Grip, startled, flew to the top of the stable.

"He's mean, that pony," said Topping.

"Not a bit of meanness in him," said Jemmy. "Not a bit of meanness at all. Why, he knows everything about my voice, he does."

"I can see that," said Topping, as Whisker made his way leisurely out of the unlocked stable door and put his head comfortably and comforting on Jemmy's shoulder.

"Good fellow, Whisker," he said. "Best old pony in the world, Whisker. Best old pony."

Jemmy saw the glint of Grip at the top of the stable. Grip poised himself suddenly, as a singer might, then let out a large "Hee-haw, hee-haw."

"You hear that, Topping? Grip taught himself that, he did. Just took his caw and changed it into hee-haw, just like a donkey. Learned it from the costermonger's donkey."

"Clever," said Topping in disgust. "Clever. All the brains in animals these days."

Whisker certainly thought so; and it was Whisker that was always to be the raven's greatest competition.

After a respectable length of time, Whisker admitted to Grip's existence—at least to the hee-haw, which Grip found could hold Whisker's attention.

That in itself was a major feat, because Whisker was a remarkably inattentive pony.

Topping gave him up in disgust.

"Jemmy, I tell you, that is a contrary pony."

"I guess we all are at times, sir," said Jemmy.

"That's the trouble with you Scots," mumbled Topping, "always a bit of the philosophy. That philosophy stuff and nonsense doesn't fit into a stable."

"I don't know about that," said Charles Dickens as he came into the stable with all the bluster and sharp look of an old stagecoachman . . . a type of man Dickens idealized.

He's like an actor himself, thought Jemmy—always dressing up in costume.

"Good morning, Topping. Good morning, Jemmy. Good morning, Grip. Good morning, Whisker."

Topping and Jemmy tipped their hats. Grip began to trumpet, "Hee-haw, hee-haw."

"Do my ears deceive me, Topping?" asked Dickens.

"Not at all, sir. But begging your pardon, sir, the stable does seem filled with young philosophers and donkeys now."

"Very clever, Grip," said Dickens. "And don't I get a greeting from you, Whisker?"

"Hold tight to your hat, sir," said Topping. "That may be the only greeting you get."

With great aloofness, Whisker turned his head to bestow a small, attentive glance on Grip, who was tumbling about in a corvine frenzy, trying to maintain the pony's attention.

Eventually, Whisker would learn to mouth a piece of straw, bend, and tease Grip with it—a piece of play that would go on indefinitely.

Ravens are "loners," but even such a loner as Grip enjoyed friendship. And if Grip masqueraded as a donkey for Whisker, Whisker soon became an enormous but dumb raven playmate to Grip.

All that was to come in time. For the moment, Dickens had come to the stable to relate his daily miseries to Whisker.

The very day before, on his maiden trip with the cart, Dickens had come a cropper with Whisker.

If you asked the pony to stop, he would not stop. He would only accede to your request from acute fatigue or if he ran into a stone wall.

In those early days, the only person whom Whisker did like was Jemmy.

Jemmy did not mind when the pony ran off at a sharp angle to inspect a lamppost on one side of any street he went down, and then went off on a tangent to inspect another lamppost on the other side. Whisker seemed to have a real need to satisfy himself about the world. He had to verify the fact that two such lampposts, for example, were of the same pattern and material. And then suddenly, unexpectedly (certainly it had happened to Dickens and always happened to Topping), Whisker would stop in his own time, apparently absorbed in his own meditation.

Grip had always had that gift of being able to look aloof, meditating on his own problems, but Whisker, four-legged, slower, no creature of mystery (no pony has anything of the supernatural about him), became even more able to absorb himself in meditation at any time. He could meditate in the middle of the street, in the middle of the garden, in the middle of the square, halfway out of his stable.

Indeed, Dickens often appealed to Whisker—just to move would mean so much. But he was as immovable as a donkey upon occasion.

"You naughty Whisker. Fie on you. I'm ashamed of such conduct."

Nothing mattered. He could not be appealed to in this way except for a brief moment. Then he would trot for a minute in a sulky manner.

Young Jemmy gradually changed all this. He knew just how to dress when he was to take the pony out. Whisker used to wait patiently for him to put on that last touch, that stiff and shiny hat, which, whenever Jemmy struck it with his knuckles, sounded like a drum. That drum sound always made Whisker come to attention.

Yes, this was Jemmy, the true master. Here was a small, important somebody, dressed in a coat of pepper and salt with a waistcoat of canary yellow. Here was his master in the luster of a new pair of boots, and here was that wonderful, wonderful hat, and the sounding of the drum in the hat. Whisker could not help coming to attention.

There continued to be slight difficulty in catching Whisker. Once Whisker managed to dodge around the small paddock in the rear, being chased by Topping, for one hour and three quarters. Topping could not understand it. Jemmy would simply go into the garden, play the drum sound on his hat, and there was Whisker, standing at attention like a good soldier.

And there was Grip! "Hee-haw, hee-haw."

And there was Dickens! Laughing.

8
Mr. Charles Dickens Falls in Love with the Queen

THE QUEEN, God bless her! The toast was on everyone's lips in those early months of 1840.

Queen Victoria of England had been only eighteen years old when she came to the throne in 1837. All the world had been fascinated by how perfectly collected and coolly dignified she had appeared to those who told her that early morning—it was just five o'clock—that she must put aside her youth and inexperience and usher in a new age.

The emissaries had knocked several times before they could rouse the porter at the gate; then they were kept waiting in the courtyard. Finally, they had to request an audience with Her Royal Highness on business of utmost importance.

The young princess was in a deep sleep. She should not be disturbed.

She must be disturbed.

"We are come on business of state to the Queen, and even her sleep must give way to that."

And so entered the Queen—a shy, young girl in a loose white nightgown and shawl, her hair falling upon her shoulders, her feet in slippers, tears in her eyes. A girl princess who had awakened a queen.

Now that same young queen had married her German cousin Albert on that momentous day, the 10th of February, 1840.

All London was talking about the marriage.

"Not sure I approve," said Cook, throwing some batter about as though she were shaking up the throne.

"She's too young, and he's too German."

"She's the Queen," said Topping. "Stubborn, I hear."

"It's a mystery," said Ella. "I didn't think royalty had measles. Didn't they say she was going to have measles?"

"She didn't have measles," said Cook, the side of her hand coming down in a knife-sharp chop on the dough. "Just a young girl's nervousness and aggravation, that's all. And she's not the only one aggravated," said Cook knowingly.

Neither Ella nor Topping said anything. They knew Cook was talking about Mr. Dickens. He was acting strangely.

"Says he's in love with the Queen," said Topping.

"Imagine," said Ella. "It's a mystery. Some people!"

"Off his feed, I'll say that," said Cook.

"Not you, not you, Grip!" Cook screamed, chasing him with a tea towel. "You're the greedy one. Master could take a lesson from you. Lets his tea get cold, he does."

"Grip likes cold tea," said Jemmy, his face and hands newly washed and crisply chapped from the cold February weather. "Grip likes his tea cold, Cook, but I like mine hot."

"You're getting to be as much a nuisance as that bird," said Cook. "Look at him now." Cook brought her apron up to her face to cover her smile. It would not do if the world knew she quite enjoyed the little devil. The rest of them said she really didn't hear him correctly, but he said it quite distinctly.

"Cook," cried the raven.

Then again, just as clear. "Cook."

"Listen," she said, turning to Ella. "Listen how he says 'Cook.' "

"Says 'caw,' " said Topping, blowing on his hot tea.

"Says 'Cook' plainly," said Cook.

" 'Caw,' " said Topping.

At this strange birdlike sound from Topping, Grip stood stock-still.

Then he began a wild dance, all the time eyeing Topping with, as Cook noted, a nice insolence of manner. The raven held his head to one side, twisting it as though he might screw it off someday.

Then very clearly (and Cook smiled to herself), impertinently, Grip placed himself in front of Topping.

"Cook," said Grip.

"All right, all right," said Topping, pushing his chair from the table. "I'm off to pick up Mr. Forster. No time for ravens."

It was John Forster, sometimes lawyer, sometimes reporter, who would be Charles Dickens' confidant and, later, biographer. It was he who recorded Dickens' wild behavior at the time of the Queen's marriage.

"I am utterly lost in misery," Dickens wrote Forster, "and can do nothing. I have been reading *Oliver*, *Pickwick*, and *Nickleby* to get my thoughts together for the new effort, but all in vain:

> "My heart is at Windsor,
> My heart isn't here;
> My heart is at Windsor,
> Afollowing my dear."

He would do anything for the Queen to notice him. Anything. Poison himself. Hang himself from the pear tree in the garden. Fall under the feet of cab horses in the New-road.

"I am sorry to add that I have fallen hopelessly in love with the Queen."

9
Ella Changes Her Mind

"STUPID BIRD. Stupid bird," said Ella, picking up one of the double damask napkins and waving it at Grip's beak. "Stupid bird. No wonder the master has lost interest in you. Dirty old thing! Go away!"

Grip lurched away. If one could say a bird was downtrodden and disappointed, rejected, it was shown in the way Grip walked away from her. Everyone had noticed that his beak, feathers, indeed his whole demeanor had drooped since the master had turned so inward upon himself. Why, Mr. Dickens hardly spoke to Grip anymore (nor to anyone else, really. Even Cook was complaining that he never "put her out" with some last-minute demand for a "collation" from the kitchen).

Now Ella wondered whether she had hurt his feelings. How ridiculous! Hurt a bird's feelings? Yet the bird did seem to try at times—to try to understand her, even to try to learn new words. Funny the way he learned some words. "Come back here, Grip," she said, and Grip turned around, lurching as though he were caught in the high spring wind that cried outside. "Come back here, Grip."

Grip looked at her, staring with those eyes.

It's those eyes that frighten you, she said to herself. That's what makes him look like a strange being. Magic birds, they said they were.

"Now try this, Grip. Polly, put the kettle on. Polly, put the

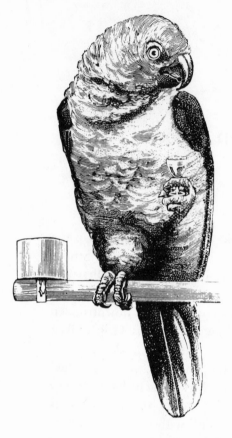

Polly, put the kettle on

BINGLEY

kettle on, and we'll all have tea. Now, my old da had a parrot that could say that. Are you as smart as a parrot, Grip?"

Grip looked at her and looked away. He made the sound that he so often did, like somebody pulling a champagne cork. Pop, pop, pop.

"Well, that's one letter," she said. "Try it again. Polly. Polly, put the kettle on, and we'll all have tea."

"Pop, pop, pop," said Grip, and flew up to the transom of the door.

"Stupid bird," said Ella, and went downstairs.

"Stupid girl," said Cook, who came upon her. "Stupid girl talking to a bird like that. You never find me talking to him."

"I'm a devil," said Grip suddenly. "I'm a devil."

"You are a devil, you," she said. "Get out of here."

Until Dickens seemed to lose interest in him, Grip's education was proceeding at a pace that pleased him, and for that matter, pleased his master.

There had been long years when there had been no pets at all in the Dickens home. For the rest of his life Dickens was to make up for it. "They called me raven-mad, did they?" Even now, struggling to start a new book, he was raven-glad to have Grip. He had never found a more responsive pet—even the white rats at school.

It's true that the nursery crowd—Kate, the babies, the babies' nurse—were none too fond of Grip, but that was natural, he supposed. It seemed to be that all pets chose one person in the household and gave nearly their all to that person; for the rest it was just sufferance. They tolerated the rest of the household. They would not be particularly negative, but on the other hand there was no true bond of understanding.

Now Grip, Dickens had noticed, put up with Topping in the stable, but truly enjoyed Jemmy, who seemed to have a natural way with all animals.

Dickens could not but notice that Jemmy had a certain fear of Grip, as though he had seen too many of those supernatural corbies in the glens of Scotland. And Ella—well, Grip seemed to enjoy tormenting Ella. He had overheard Ella once saying, "Dirty bird," but he knew Grip to be an extremely clean bird, using what proper facilities a good Victorian bird would use, and always preening and cleaning those shining black feathers.

Cook, of course, Grip adored, and Dickens was fascinated with the barely concealed delight that appeared on Cook's face when Grip looked at her and unmistakably, yes, unmistakably said, "Halloa, old girl."

"Cook beamed," said Dickens, and it had become Grip's favorite expression.

In this period, however, when Dickens was feeling his way into a new book, he was either away or so withdrawn in the library that a kind of silence settled over the house. The silence entered even Grip.

The silence was a mystery, thought Ella. Cook was gloomy; even "stupid girl" which Cook often called her was better than nothing.

Ella would be very patient and teach Grip some new words, and then the house wouldn't be so, so what? Well, miserable, that's what.

"Come here, Grip," said Ella.

Grip eyed her suspiciously.

"You want to be smarter than a parrot."

"All ravens are smarter than parrots," said Topping, coming into the warm kitchen.

"He doesn't want to talk at all," said Ella sadly. "I'm trying to teach him, 'Polly, put the kettle on.' "

"Ella, Ella, Ella," called Cook.

Ella rushed off.

"Well, say something, Grip," said Topping. "Tell Ella what you think of life."

" 'ell," said Grip.

"That's right," said Topping, burning his mouth on the tea. "Life's hell all right."

"What did you say, Topping?" said Cook, carrying a large leg of mutton like a great weapon.

"Just agreeing with Grip," said Topping, looking at the bird judiciously. "Ella just taught him to say 'ell."

Ella burst into tears. Cook, Topping, and Grip were caught like frozen statues. Ella's miseries always had that effect on people.

Grip broke the silence.

" 'ell," he cawed. " 'ell," he tried once again.

And then quite clearly, as Cook said, "Just as clear as the master himself. Grip said 'Ella.' That's what he said."

" 'ell!"

"Ella, listen," said Cook. "He's saying your own name. Stop

that infernal crying. Stop it, I say, Ella."

Ella uncovered her eyes and looked at Cook through her tears.

"Did he, Cook?"

"Of course, stupid girl."

"Smart bird," said Ella. "Smart bird."

But Grip had sailed out of the door with Topping. He always liked to try his new words on Whisker.

Whisker, with true stubborn pony aplomb, refused to acknowledge the extent of Grip's vocabulary.

"Pow, pow, pow. Pop, pop, pop. I'm a devil."

Grip danced around like a vaudeville performer, but Whisker acknowledged only his oats.

" 'ell," Grip tried, but Whisker didn't even sweep his tail.

"He's swearing," Jemmy said in awe.

"Thought so myself," said Topping. "Used to know a raven who said 'go to hell' with pleasure."

"Cook says it isn't so," said Topping, "says Grip is really saying Ella."

"Ella," said Jemmy. "Why should Grip say 'Ella'?"

"Making up to her, I suppose," said Topping in disgust. "Terrible fooler. Look at him now."

Grip had finally caught Whisker's attention with his donkey sound, "Hee-haw, hee-haw!"

Whisker dropped some oats and grinned the wicked grin that ponies sometimes affect, of great teeth and lip, that meant yes. Yes, Grip was a great donkey.

10
A Stone of Spring

GRIP had a favorite spot to take his morning ablutions. Like all British gentlemen of the nineteenth century, he liked his bath water cold and his breakfast fatty. He carried his breakfast with him. He was much more clever than the businessmen who went into the City to the great mercantile centers or even Dickens himself, who had, much to Jemmy's pleasure, journeyed to Scotland, where his readers always greeted him with enthusiasm.

It was a fine spring day—a day to be out—a day to see the world. In that way Grip was remarkably like his master.

So, gingerly carrying a very fine piece of bacon, which he had conjured from Cook, Grip began his daily adventures. Cook no longer ignored him and always left a fine piece of bacon out where he could get it with reasonable ease, muttering all the time as she did, "Easier that way, he'd get it anyway, that thief. Besides, plenty of bacon around. Likes a streak of bacon, he does. That Grip. After all, isn't life a streak of bacon? White and pink, black and white, laced with all sorts of things."

"You never do know what's going to happen, do you?" she muttered to Ella. But Ella just looked at her and said, "No, ma'am. You never know. It's a mystery."

So, gathering up his bacon, Grip took off, winging his way around the house as though he were checking on all matters of decorum, making sure that the proper windows were open, and the proper doors closed, making sure that the vines were growing, that the leaves were coming out properly, that the spring bulbs were showing a tint of green, making sure, as he flew through the stable, that Jemmy was at work, as he often was, grooming the pony, making sure that Whisker and he, Grip, were still at odds. They looked each other in the eye, Whisker spattering Jemmy with hay as though he were some political speaker who had a lot to say and couldn't say it fast enough, and Grip for once, showing his own disapproval by spattering Jemmy's black "drummer" hat with bacon bits.

"Get out of here, you bird. Get! Get! Get out of here, you bird! You see what he did, Topping?"

"Those that keeps birds must get trouble," said Topping wisely. "Smart bird."

After Grip had inspected all corners of the stable and the corners in the greenhouse, after he had sat for a moment beside old Patterson, the gardener, he knew he had done his duty. "A regular policeman making the rounds, aren't you, Grip? What's the name of that fellow who comes to see the master? A regular Mr. Inspector Stalker. You think you're a detective, the way you're looking around."

And, in answer to that particular conversation, Grip did indeed seem to take long, dark looks immediately around him.

But he must be off. Even the most important of London characters must be off. He must be off and have his breakfast, which he still held, relishing the slim sliver of fat, as it went down his throat. Grip was off to take his ablutions. The Dickenses had long before put in that unbelievable phenomenon of the nineteenth century—a private bathroom. It was the talk of the downstairs.

"Never such nonsense," said Cook. "Bit of a wash, a cleanup, each one in a private room, ridiculous! What's things coming to?"

"Nonsense itself," said Ella. "A mystery. Strange they didn't make one for the bird." And then she let out one of her peculiar laughs. "Ha, ha, ha." When she did that, if he was around, Grip did the same thing. "Ha, ha, ha."

"The two of you," Cook would then say, "the two of you. Strange birds you are, Ella. You and your ha, ha, ha."

But Grip was not around, and Ella's ha, ha, ha fell flat. No, poor Grip did not have a bathroom of his own, but he had singled out one himself, and it was a dandy one indeed. High, clean, coolish in the morning, and the greatest spot for ablutions, outside of the seashore, that any bird could want.

Grip had picked it out early in his sojourn at the Dickens establishment. It was on top of the high wall leading to the main gate. It was a shallow concave section that caught some sweet rain. In bad weather it also caught soot from the chimney. The chimney, as usual, was smoking in the direction of the neighbor, and sooner or later this would cause trouble with the neighbor. But those little bits of cinders didn't bother Grip any more than they would have bothered the chimney sweep. As a matter of fact, the chimney sweep, going past the house on his way to the beautiful houses around Regent's Park, could see Grip up there, splattering around in the early morning dew and water.

"Hey, bird, you're cleaner than I am," he said. "Hey, bird, you're cleaner than I am. Want a job? Those wings of yours would spread down a chimney beautiful-like. You've got regular brooms attached to you. Want a job?"

And then the sweep went toward the stables to see Jemmy, who always gave him a cup of tea.

Nobody worked harder. Jemmy, who was a friend to many, knew the sweep well. He often discussed the sweep's life with Dickens, who had great sympathy for sweeps. Hadn't he made Oliver Twist frightened and unbelievably terrified by the fact that he might be apprenticed to a chimney sweep? Many small boys, particularly small homeless boys, pauper boys, the smaller the better, were in the hands of bad men who needed them to climb chimneys and clean them out. Sometimes the boys fell asleep in their dark holes; some did not work rapidly enough to please their cruel masters; some burned their feet. It was no life for any boy, and Dickens must have realized it, because he could not have even

A London chimney sweep

"CHATTERBOX"

his character Oliver suffering so, but had to apprentice him to the hardly better coffinmaker before he got into the clutches of that strange employer, Fagin.

"See you, Grip," said the small sweep, waving as he left.

And Grip bounced up and down. "I'm a devil," he cried out.

"You are that," said the chimney sweep. "I'm a sweep, can you say that? Tom, the sweep."

"Ta, ta," said Grip. "Ta."

"Ta," said the sweep.

And so, appropriately enough, Grip turned to his ablutions. The rainwater was fresh and delightful. He fluttered and skittered through it, his long wings glistening with ebony sparkles in the morning light. Properly washed up, he dried off in one stone corner, where he felt protected from the wind, and devoured the rest of his waiting breakfast. If he had felt that Cook was truly an appropriate person in his scale of values, he would have congratulated her. He was, after all, a polite bird, and for the moment he seemed to hesitate. Perhaps he would fly back to the kitchen. However, sometimes his presence brought him bacon, and sometimes it brought him a broom.

Life outside in the spring was more exciting. Now he could climb up on the parapet, where he seemed almost like a statue. A black bird keeping guard over the household, over a medieval castle. If he could think, goodness knows what he would have thought. That he was a talisman of the household? a guard bird?

He stood on one leg, gazing out across Regent's Park. Regent's Park never excited him. The zoo was in Regent's Park, and Dickens went over there regularly. Grip was not even excited enought to see what was there. Or was he rather afraid of the cages? Way, way back somewhere in the dim, dark childhood of his bird life there had been a cage, but now there was never a cage. There was his basket, if he wanted to get into it, the stable, and for the rest, his strange, wild semihuman life.

"I'm a devil," he said to himself. "I'm a devil." He might have said he had it easy. And certainly he was a presence there, as he

The zoo in Regent's Park

DORÉ

stood that day, carefree, proud of himself, his great wings stretched out, fluttering almost like a windmill, his black feathers glistening, shedding a feather or two. He had done this before, and once Ainsworth, the great writer, had picked up one of those raven feathers and made a witch's chant:

> Adder's skin and raven's feather,
> With shell of beetle blent together,
> By this strong suffumigation,
> By this potent invocation,
> Spirits! I compel you here!

But this morning Grip just stood there, rippling his feathers, letting out just plain friendly caws to the milkman who went by in the cart. He was alert to all the daily activities of the street—the woman selling lavender, the boy selling muffins, the girl selling cherries.

He did not notice an approaching gang of ruffians. Nobody knew quite what they were doing, but suddenly out of nowhere a great stone flew up and hit Grip. It caught him on the wing. He tried desperately to flutter and hold his own, but he could not.

"Gad, you got him," the boys said. "Let's capture him."

"No, let's get away from here. Come, fast!"

And the gardener came sweeping out from nowhere.

"Get away, you boys! That's Grip. That's Grip."

But Grip could hear nothing. He could feel himself falling. Falling. How strange to fall and not have your wings to hold you up. Falling, falling to the ground, with one of those great, black, beautiful wings crushed and limp as a dirty paintbrush.

11
The Convalescent

"GIVE him to me. I'll try to make the poor beast comfortable," said Cook, stretching out her hands for Grip.

"I tried to find the bird fancier," said Jemmy. "He's great with animals. Said he'd always be around. But he wasn't."

"Well, it's words and actions, and actions and words. Different things at times," said Cook. "Come on. Hand him over. Many a bird I've handled."

"I know that," said Jemmy, "but you generally wind up cooking them."

"Nobody's ever cooked a raven yet," said Cook. "Don't be silly. I'll cure the beast, I will. Won't be the first one I've done."

Grip was still lying there unconscious, his wing curiously crumbled. This Beau Brummel, always so highly glossed that he might have been, with proper top hat and coat, ready to go out to Covent Garden in his glistening black feathers, was now anything but a dandy. He was a dismal, almost shaggy, bird. One eye was half-closed; the other, at the sound of Cook's voice, opened, but did not give her the usual imperious stare. Cook looked down on him and said, "Poor thing. Poor beast." And Grip shuddered.

Perhaps this reaction from Cook was just too much for him. But he seemed to straighten out.

"He's not going to die, is he?" shouted Ella. "Oh, not here, not in the kitchen. Get him out in the stable if he's going to die. I don't want dead things in the kitchen."

"Now, do be quiet, Ella," said Cook, taking command. "Do be quiet and fetch me a proper box and some cotton batting."

"It's a mystery. It's a mystery," yelled Ella, knocking over a chair.

"Now, don't wake up the mistress," said Cook. "This probably never would have happened if the master wasn't away. I'm not so sure I approve of that, leaving those young children so often. He may be London's greatest writer, but is he a proper father to three little mites like that? And another on the way. That's what is the matter. Grip was missing the master."

"He's more than a bit mean to the children," said Ella. "None of them likes the way he nips ankles."

"Just a show of affection," said Cook. "Just a show of affection. I've grown quite used to it."

"That's because he can barely find your ankles," said Jemmy. "They're so wrapped up in all those aprons of yours, he's just biting on a piece of white cloth. He doesn't know any better."

"Poor Grip. That's enough of that, Jemmy. Just plain freshness, that is. What's the matter with you, lad, you look like you've been crying."

"I am indeed, ma'am. I cried when I picked him up. He seemed like such a special bird. You know like he was a very, very special bird, indeed. And he reminded me of my old dog."

"Well, you've got an almost dog out in the stable now. You've almost turned that wild pony into a dog. Whisker! Whoever called a pony Whisker? Whiskey would have been better. Always acted to me as though that pony had more than a dram in him before he takes off. Never knows quite where he's going or if he knows where you're going, decides to turn around and go the other way. Shocking manners for a pony! Did you get that box, Ella? Now, give it to me. That's a good girl. Hold it steady. Now, put the cotton batting in, and there, I'll put him in the box."

"Ow-w-w," yelled Ella in a mournful cry. "Ow-w-w."

"What are you yelling for now?" said Cook. "He's not dead yet."

"Probably will be," said Ella. "Hard to keep a bird alive, one with a broken wing like that, and goodness knows what else is the matter with him."

"Just a little heartsick, that's what I think. A little heartsick. Topping, do you know where that port is?"

"Who me?" asked Topping.

"I'm not accusing you, Topping. I just said, do you know where that port is? Get a little. I'll give him just a tiny drop."

"He'll be a drunken bird," said Jemmy. "We don't want a drunken bird on our hands."

"He won't be a drunken bird, the way I do it. He'll just be a bird warm and comfortable by the big stove with just a wee drop in him. Now, go get the port."

They all stood over Grip, and, if Grip sensed their presence, he tried to ignore it. He opened neither eye, nor stubbornly, would he open his beak.

"Come, come, Grip. Come, come. Where's that popping noise you make? Where's that popping noise? One pop, and I could pop this port right down your throat."

But Grip lay silent.

"I never thought I'd complain about this bird, that he was so silent," said Cook. "Such a nuisance, he's been. Such a nuisance, he with his 'I'm a devil,' hop, hop, hopping all over the place. What are we to do now, Topping?"

Topping stood there, scratching his head with one hand and holding a somewhat bedraggled cap in the other.

"Birds is not my business. Horses is my business. What do you think, Jemmy?"

"Well, horses is my business, too. Aren't they, Topping? Birds is not my business."

"Don't just be imitating me," said Topping. "You're more of a country boy than I ever was. You must know something about birds."

"I don't know," said Jemmy. "Must make me think of my old

dog. Not the one in the stable. My old dog. Oh, that was awful. Old Bronty, we called him. Never forget the time he died. My family stood around and looked like all of April was coming down our cheeks, we were weeping so. Oh, what a grand dog he was. I don't know why Grip reminds me of him so much, except Bronty was the color of a raven, you see. Black, black as a raven. Purple-black just like Grip, he was. All over. Except, I remember, it wasn't just that; he had one star right on his breast. A strange star. Oh, what a great dog he was. And how strong he was, and wise, and yet you felt there was a fierceness deep down inside him. Still, when he laid his head upon your knee and lifted his eyes to you, you wouldn't think he was a dog at all, but very intellectual, and a moral creature. If something happened, if it was you that were in danger, he would have torn a lion in pieces. But to a child, he was wonderful then. I could hang by his mane, play with his fangs, even. Never a worry did anybody have about any child coming near old Bronty."

"What happened to him?" said Cook.

"Some devil just poisoned him, he did. I always thought there was nothing worse than the poisoning of a dog."

"Well, murder's murder," said Topping. "Doesn't matter how it comes. Whether it's two feet or four feet, that's a murder. That's a terrible crime, an awful crime. I often wonder if the birds and beasts and insects have mortal souls."

"Well, come along with you now," said Cook. "Poor Grip will be having a mortal death himself unless we warm him up a little now. Get one of those best napkins all folded up. That's right, Ella. Now, put it over him."

Ella put forth a loud laugh that was nearly as bad as her mournful cry. "Doesn't he look funny? Like some old schoolteacher, or a dunce. Put a paper cap on his head, and he'd look like a dunce."

"You're the dunce," said Cook. "You're the dunce."

"Oh, look, Cook. He's opened his eyes."

"So he has," said Cook. "So he has. It's the warmth and the good conversation that's around him. He was always a bird that liked good conversation. He'll do all right now. He'll be all right. Won't you, Grip?"

And very feebly and far away came a small "Pop."

12
A Collation

"COOK, Cook," shouted Dickens down the hatchway of the dining room.

"Listen to him," said Cook. "He's got his spirits back. Both of them—Grip and the master."

"All over the place," grumbled Ella.

"Maybe the party last night. Mr. Maclise always cheers him up," said Cook. "I think I'll just see what the master has to say."

"Feels like ten o'clock at night," said Ella. "And the day's just started."

"Not his day," said Cook, straightening up her cap and smoothing out the pink ribbons. "Master's been up since way before dawn, walking."

"Just look at that service-lift," said Ella. "A mountain of crumbs, dirty plates, scraps of lobster. . ."

At the sound of lobster, Grip came out of nowhere and grabbed the shell.

"No, Grip, no," shouted Ella. She sat down and started to cry—a piercing cry.

"Are we giddy down here, too?" said Dickens, tapping out a brisk tattoo on the downstairs steps.

All looked up in surprise. Cook bobbed side to side like a large dumpling, and curtsied.

"I was about to come up, sir."

"Excellent dinner party, Cook. Mr. Maclise sent his compliments. And tonight you'll have competition."

"Competition?" said Cook.

"Tonight he dines with the Queen."

"The Queen, sir!" Cook wrapped one of the pink ribbons around her finger in embarrassment.

"I vouch he prefers your cooking. And Ella? What ails Ella? Are you haunted by the ghost of dinner parties past?"

"It's the bird, sir. Stole a lobster claw."

"Ah, an aristocratic bird, indeed," said Dickens. "Yes, you can always tell a bird by the company he keeps. Grip, come to the library. Drop that, Grip."

Grip dropped the shell.

"It's the smell, sir," said Ella. "He's always hiding things, sir."

How jolly the kitchen looked in the daytime, thought Dickens. He could vaguely remember his grandmother in a kitchen like this, wielding all the authority of Cook. She, too, had such ribbons in her hair, and such pink cheeks, and skillful fingers.

Dickens' own grandmother, by the time Dickens was a young boy, had lived, however, in grand retirement (or so it seemed to the young boy). A servant she might have been, *but*, and Dickens comforted himself with the idea, her service had been with the mighty in the land. Eventually, she was housekeeper to the great Baron Crewe.

Cook's kitchen looked so comfortable. There was a blazing fire. Half the floor was covered with an old oilcloth; the other half had naked flagstone. And look at that table—a magnificent uncut ham, with a great quartern loaf of bread, nine eggs (why nine? wondered Dickens), two magnificent pyramids of muffins, a dozen ship biscuits, half a pork pie, a dozen kidneys spluttering on the spit before the fire, and a young kitchen maid, speechless but with a very red face, holding a gridiron with mutton chops.

Dickens suddenly felt very young. He longed to sit down at that table and have a grilled chop, a kidney. But that simply was not done. Upstairs and downstairs never mixed at table.

"For dinner, Cook," he said, "a collation . . ."

"I know just what you want, sir," said Cook, curtseying again.

"Yes, you do, Cook. A savory pie oozing at the corners, and a deviled grill and kidney. In the library. It's back to work. Come, Grip."

"Wonderful," said Cook to herself. "He's back to himself, he is. A collation. . ."

Then Cook heard him call from the shaft of the service-lift.

"And, Cook, Cook, could you manage a small plate of beef a la mode to eat with it?"

Why that? thought Cook.

But Dickens knew. There had been a time when a small plate of beef a la mode had taken away the sting of being so rejected by his parents in those unhappy years when he had been sent to work two days after his twelfth birthday.

The beef pie had been given to him in lodgings he thought were paradise.

Paradise! Charles Dickens remembered those days well.

There was a paradise of lodging with a paradise of a family on Lark Street in London. The landlord was a charming old fellow— fat, good-natured, and very, very kind. He had a quiet but charming old wife and a very innocent grown-up son who was lame as was his father.

That happy family deserved to be remembered, to be re-created, and Charles Dickens was doing just that as he sat down each morning to work on the novel that he had finally decided to call *The Old Curiosity Shop.*

So many bits and pieces of the past had combined together in his mind to inspire that story. There had been that day only recently—it was dawn really, barely sunrise, with the first touch of spring, when he had been walking through Covent Garden Market. The flower scents were heavy in the air, and suddenly he heard the sound of a dusky thrush.

Dickens often walked through Covent Garden Market

DORÉ

He thought suddenly of the wild freedom of the birds, of the peculiar and delightful independence of Grip. He had been neglecting Grip recently, and when he did, the bird managed to have an accident.

The song of the thrush came from overhead, and Dickens looked up, startled, to see that the thrush, singing as if he were mad with joy, was caged.

Poor bird, he thought, poor birds; there were such captives all through Covent Garden Market. Caged birds gave the poor of London a vision of the country—but often the captives were mistreated; they lay drooping in the spring light.

The new book had been inspired by captive birds, by the vision of a beautiful child he had seen in Bath on a trip with Forster, by a misshapen villain, whom Dickens curiously identified with himself, by the strange old shops that always caught his fancy in London.

All of nineteenth-century Londontown had strange odd corners, and often he wandered into those shops which had all sorts of curious things for sale. He had remembered those shops from the time he was living with the jolly little landlord, while his parents were still living in prison.

What an odd life it had been for young Dickens. He slept at the Garlands' (the name he would give his happy family), and then bright and early he would breakfast "at home." At home was Marshalsea Prison, where he could see his family. This arrangement was not unusual for many bankrupt families.

Not only Charles but also the maid of all work, an orphan from the Chatham workhouse, both arrived at the gates of the prison at sunrise. Poor as his parents were, the orphan girl continued to serve them in prison—often arriving there accompanied by Charles, who frightened her with tales of ghosts and spirits and astonishing fiction about the grand old town of London. That orphan girl, too, would appear in *The Old Curiosity Shop*, as the Marchioness, the sharp and worldly small servant.

Sometimes Charles would accompany her to her lodgings at

night, pointing out the fascinating shops—shops that contained suits of mail standing like ghosts, fantastic carvings, distorted figures in china and wood and iron, tapestries and strange furniture that might have been made from dreams.

The characters that Dickens needed had come to him from the past and the present. He wrote with speed and pleasure— writing in serial form, so that he did not know from one week to the next what aspects of his story lay ahead of him, or even what people he might meet who would inspire him further; or, for that matter, what animal friend.

On those late spring mornings, he looked from the library window to the front of the stable, where Whisker basked sleepily in the sun. Grip joined Dickens at the window. The raven, Dickens observed, was in a highly reflective state, walking up and down the windowsill with an air of elderly complacency that was strongly suggestive of his having his hands under his coattails. He would stop, look out the window, and inspect a shadow on the lawn.

The shadow turned out to be Ella, combing her hair with the silver comb given to her by Dickens.

Grip stropped his beak upon the windowsill and cried out in his hoarse tones, "I'm a devil, I'm a devil, I'm a devil."

But whether he addressed his observations to Ella, or merely threw them off as a general remark, Dickens felt was a matter of uncertainty.

Such reflections were interrupted by the arrival from the kitchen of a superb beef a la mode.

Dickens took a large white napkin and draped it around Grip's neck. The bird looked like a very distinguished waiter. His master said, "Manners, Grip, manners," and the bird stood stock-still while he was rewarded with a small saucer of gravy.

"Gravy," said Cook later. "Grip likes gravy, indeed. There is no such passion in human nature as the passion for gravy among gentlemen. But birds! I tell you, Ella, the gravy I've cooked in my

years! But gravy for a bird—it's enough, Ella, to add twenty years
to one's age."

"It's a mystery," said Ella.

"Is there any more?" said Jemmy, coming in.

"More what?" said Cook.

"Gravy."

"Birds of a feather," said Cook. "Here's your gravy."

Then she sat down and wiped her face with a clean white
towel.

"Presiding over an establishment like this," said Cook when
she appeared once again from behind the towel, "presiding over
an establishment like this makes sad havoc with the features. No
one would believe," and she looked around the room, ignoring
Jemmy and Ella, looking, Jemmy supposed, for No One, "yes, no
one would believe . . . the . . . passion . . . for . . . gravy."

13
Stop, Thief!

"STOP, thief!"

It was a woman's voice. Jemmy and Whisker both put their ears on the alert, but it seemed to Jemmy that it came from a distance.

"Stop, thief!"

Was it a little closer now?

That was always a cry that put everybody in Victorian London on the alert. Dickens had the best to say about it, thought Jemmy, right on that page of *Oliver Twist* which he had memorized along with many others:

> " 'Stop thief! Stop thief!' There is a magic in the sound. The tradesman leaves his counter, and the car-man his waggon; the butcher throws down his tray; the baker his basket; the milkman his pail; the errand-boy his parcels; the school-boy his marbles; the paviour his pickaxe; the child his battledore. Away they run, pell-mell, helter-skelter, slap-dash: tearing, yelling, screaming, knocking down the passengers as they turn the corners, rousing up the dogs, and astonishing the fowls: and streets, squares, and courts, re-echo with the sound.
> " 'Stop thief! Stop thief!' The cry is taken up by a hundred voices, and the crowd accumulate at every turning. Away they fly, splashing through the mud, and rattling along the pavements: up go the windows, out run the people, onward bear the mob, a whole audience desert Punch in the very thickest of the plot, and, joining the rushing throng, swell the

shout, and lend fresh vigour to the cry, 'Stop thief! Stop thief!'

" 'Stop thief! Stop thief!' There is a passion *for hunting something* deeply implanted in the human breast. One wretched, breathless child, panting with exhaustion; terror in his looks; agony in his eyes; large drops of perspiration streaming down his face; strains every nerve to make head upon his pursuers; and as they follow on his track, and gain upon him every instant, they hail his decreasing strength with still louder shout, and whoop and scream with joy. 'Stop thief!' Ay, stop him for God's sake, were it only in mercy!"

But, yes, this time the cry was nearer.

"Jemmy," screamed Ella.

Jemmy dropped Whisker's reins and stared up at the house. Ella was hanging from the back window, her long black hair so shielding her face that she looked like one of those witches on Jemmy's own Scottish heath.

"Bubble, bubble," muttered Jemmy to himself, in no hurry to follow Ella's interminable orders. Cook had gone down to Broadstairs to establish the Dickens family in their seashore lodgings for the summer, and Ella, well, Ella thought she was the mistress of all she surveyed.

"Jemmy, come up here!"

"All right, all right," Jemmy yelled back. He could feel Whisker's dismay. Whisker never took any orders from anyone who shouted at him. He turned his large, shocked eyes at Jemmy. Don't go, he seemed to say.

"Well, sometimes you have to," said Jemmy, a little embarrassed that he had to explain himself to a pony. The pony was equally embarrassed. He hung his head, staring in a despondent

Looking for thieves in Dickens' London

DORÉ

way at the splotch of sunlight at his feet. "I'll only be a minute. I'm not going to rush for her."

Whisker turned his eyes again on Jemmy. The eyes seemed full of shame.

"Stop, thief!"

Both Whisker and Jemmy looked up at the window.

Why, that was Ella calling, "Stop, thief!"

"Coming," screamed Jemmy, bounding up steps and attic stairs. "Coming," he called at each jump. "Coming, Ella, coming, coming."

Ella stood in the door of her tiny room, bracing herself, but with Jemmy before her, she dropped her arms and mimicked Cook's favorite pose—both hands on hips.

"Didn't you hear me call, Jemmy? Where is everyone? I called from the front windows, I called from the side windows, I called *you!*"

"I thought it was an errand," said Jemmy, hot and uncomfortable. He didn't see any signs of a thief as he looked cautiously around the room.

"I didn't know you were the one calling, 'Stop, thief!' Where is he?"

"What do you mean, where is he?"

"Where's the thief?"

"Gone," moaned Ella. "And not a one to help me. Cook and Topping at Broadstairs. Not a constable on the beat. And you . . ." Ella's disgust was such that she could not finish the sentence.

"Easy," said Jemmy. Whisker always responded to easy; so did the coach horses.

"Easy."

It worked. Ella grew calmer.

"Now, tell me," said Jemmy, pleased at how effective one simple word could be, "now tell me, Ella, just what happened." He should have known it.

"It's a mys—" and then Ella broke into tears.

"Easy," Jemmy tried again. "Easy, Ella, tears never yet wound up a clock, or worked a steam engine."

At this startling piece of information, Ella parted her hair from where it curtained her face and stared out at Jemmy as though she had never seen him before.

"What's it got to do with clocks?" said Ella. "What's it got to do with steam engines?"

Jemmy decided it was better not to explain. Maybe if he didn't say anything, Ella wouldn't burst into tears again.

But, yes, she could. Ella had, as Cook said, a very genius for tears. She, Cook, was a genius in the kitchen; Topping and Jemmy had a genius for horses; and Ella—well, Ella had a genius for tears.

Ella stared at Jemmy, and, slowly, from the pit of her soul, two round fat tears struggled out of her eyes. It was like priming a pump, and Jemmy watched with fascination. In barely a second the water main that must have been buried deep in Ella's head(?), heart(?)—Jemmy wasn't sure—gave way, and Ella broke forth into lamentations.

"Oh, oh, oh. My, my, my. Woe, woe, woe. My comb, my comb."

"What?" said Jemmy, interested now despite himself.

"It was such a sunny day," sobbed Ella.

"You can't cry and talk at the same time," said Jemmy. That happened to be untrue, thought Jemmy. Ella could. She had a genius for it. But he wanted to get the facts. With Topping and Cook away, he felt suddenly in charge.

"Easy, Ella. The whole story now."

"A sunny day," sobbed Ella. "I opened the window."

"I opened all the stable," said Jemmy.

"Do you want my story, or don't you?" said Ella crossly.

"Yes," said Jemmy amiably.

"I washed my hair," said Ella.

"Looks smashing," said Jemmy.

"Do you really think so?" said Ella. Perhaps Jemmy was a decent sort after all.

"I combed my hair," said Ella, but to this piece of fascinating information Jemmy had no reply.

"I combed my hair with the silver comb that the master gave me on Boxing Day."

"It is a nice comb," said Jemmy.

"Was, was, was," said Ella, and started to cry again.

"Was, was, was, what?" said Jemmy.

"Was a nice comb. It's gone," said Ella.

"Gone?"

"Stolen," said Ella.

"Somebody came in here and stole your comb?"

"Yes, yes," sobbed Ella. "And I shouted, 'Stop, thief! Stop, thief! Stop, thief!' "

Jemmy found himself growing pink and guilty. He should have rushed into the house immediately.

"I'll find him," said Jemmy, puffing himself. "A little rascal, I bet. A chimney sweep in the pay of some mob. Came down the chimney, robbed you, and took off like the wind."

"No," said Ella decisively. "Came in the window."

"With you here?" asked Jemmy.

"I had my back turned; the comb was on the windowsill. I heard him. Terrible sound. The sound of wings. Supernatural wings. The devil."

"The devil?" said Jemmy.

"Why, Grip, you fool. He flew in and stole my comb."

"Grip?" said Jemmy, and, almost in shock, he turned and walked down the stairs. "Grip, she said," and Jemmy found himself laughing.

Grip the rascal. Grip the devil. The bird Grip.

14
Accusations

JEMMY made only a halfhearted effort to find Grip.

"What am I supposed to do, Whisker? Fly? And how do you punish a bird anyway?"

Whisker thought this question over carefully. He raised his eyes as though calling upon the Almighty for help. And then, being a very mundane pony, went back to his oats.

"Besides, I've too much to do. And who knows it was Grip, anyway? She didn't actually see him. That's not really evidence, is it, Whisker?"

Whisker's tail beat a very solid note of approval to this way of thinking. The thud knocked more of the old paint off the stall.

"I'll have you out of here tomorrow, Whisker. The painters started in at the coach stalls today; they'll get to yours tomorrow. I'll take you to Mr. Macready's stable tomorrow. You'll have a bit of a change, you will. Just like Mr. Dickens himself down there in Broadstairs. And Topping will be back, and Cook. How do you like that?"

But there was no reply from Whisker and no sign of Grip.

And Ella, well, Ella had indeed calmed down. She was sitting in the kitchen looking for all the world as if no tear had ever played havoc with her face. A policeman had finally caught up with the whereabouts of Ella's call for "Stop, thief," and when it was discovered that it had emerged from the house of Mr. Dickens, the famous writer—and a friend of the Detective

71

Inspector himself—well, Ella had become a person of prominence.

The policeman, Constable Hunt was his name, had a very strange sense of humor, Jemmy discovered.

"Now, you, sir, my lad, how recently, sir, did you see the perpetrator?"

"Constable Hunt is one of the gentlemen"—Ella put a careful emphasis on the word "gentlemen"—"that captured Tally-ho Thompson."

"The horse thief," said Jemmy, looking up in surprise.

"The very same," said Constable Hunt. "Tally-ho Thompson. Very good tea, miss, very good tea, indeed. Tally-ho Thompson the same, horse stealer and magsman. Found him in a park (after much detective work). I put my hand upon his shoulder this way—"

And Constable Hunt put his hand upon Jemmy's considerably lower shoulder, and Jemmy felt the terrible weight of the law.

"Just like that," said Constable Hunt. "Then I looked him in the eyes, just like this . . ."

Jemmy didn't like the eyes of the law either. They were large, wet, knowing eyes.

"Go on, Officer," said Ella, pouring so much more tea that it overflowed the policeman's cup.

"I looked him in the eye, sir, and I said, 'Tally-ho Thompson, it's no use. I know you. I'm an officer from London, and I take you into custody for felony'! 'That be damned,' says Tally-ho Thompson. And you, sir," said Constable Hunt, pressing Jemmy's shoulder tighter. "And you, sir. Suppose I was to say, sir, it's no use. I'm an officer from headquarters, and I take you into custody for stealing one silver comb. What would you say, sir?"

Jemmy's blood ran cold. It was still possible in Victorian London that the theft of a silver comb could mean imprisonment. Indeed, a few short decades ago, it could have meant death.

"But, Officer!" cried Ella. "It wasn't Jemmy. It was Grip."

"I realize that," said the policeman. "But one has to be *sure* it *was* this so-called perpetrator, Grip," and he turned back to his tea.

Jemmy could feel the sweat run down his back. He had been accused unjustly. Suppose Grip had been, too? Besides, where was Grip, anyway?

Jemmy went back to the stable and stood trembling for a long time beside Whisker. Then he rubbed the pony down. He felt Whisker quiver under his hands as though he had picked up Jemmy's own anxiety.

"Keep your head down, Whisker!" But Whisker pawed and kept looking up to the rafters of the stable.

"Are you trying to tell me something, Whisker?" And Whisker turned on him that moist eye, so different from the eye of the policeman, an eye almost of supplication. That was enough for Jemmy. He leaped for the old ladder leading to the hayloft in the stable, scrambled up into the shadows, and waited until his eyes adjusted to the dark world. That's where he found Grip, unconscious, his beak sealed with dried paint.

15
The Bird Fancier

JEMMY gathered up Grip and ran. He ran through back gardens, coverts, alleys, and side streets, where he finally came to the house of the barber and bird fancier. Why bird vets and barbers went together as might costers and their donkeys, Jemmy didn't know, but he had met old Pol, the bird fancier, and if anyone could help, Pol could.

"Give him here," said Pol. "First, first, very first thing not to do is handle a sick bird. Put him in this box."

"What's the matter with him?"

"Paint. Curiosity. Put his beak in a paint bucket. Happens."

All the while, Pol was gently scraping the paint from Grip's beak, and when he succeeded, the bird fancier let out a large demanding "Caw."

The bird struggled, looked at Pol. Closed his eyes.

"He's alive," said Jemmy.

"Caw," said Pol again.

Grip opened one eye and looked at the tall featherless bird hovering over him.

"Caw," Grip answered Pol. One bird to another.

The small lost cry almost brought tears to Jemmy's eyes. Assured that Grip would live, he began to look around the shop. Few of the birds were caged. Suddenly old Pol began to speak to them, each in their own cry and whistle.

There was pandemonium as they answered.

London summer street scene

DORÉ

"How do you do that?" said Jemmy, fascinated.

"We'll put Grip up here on the shelf," said old Pol. "Give him some oil. Let nature take its course now. Some birds live; some die. Some live and die later. Months later.

"How do I do that?" Pol continued. "Cure sick birds? Talk to birds? Long story. Sit down. I came from a coster family. Sold vegetables along the street when I was no bigger than four. Had a caged bird though. Bird died."

"But none of your birds are caged."

"Don't believe in it. First of all, birds should never be caged. Wanted to be like the birds. Met old Mick."

"Who was old Mick?"

"Bird catcher. Started me out. Said I'd never make a good one. Started too late. Old Mick started when he was six, mind you. Don't start by six, you'll never make a bird catcher. Need a bit of the gypsy in you, he says. Helps. You've gotta be wandering the countryside, like a tinker. You go right on catching into old age. Old Mick just died. Loved it, he did. The bird-catchin'. Preferred being a bird fancier. I can doctor any bird. All kinds of them. I didn't know there were so many birds in my life until I was as old as ten. Started doctoring birds then."

Old Pol became less abrupt. He got up once or twice to look at Grip, and then, thought Jemmy, began to talk as though, like Grip, his voice had been sealed for a long time.

"Not difficult to understand birds. A special friend of yours?" asked Pol, nodding his head toward Grip.

"Everybody's friend," said Jemmy, "not mine especially. I'd say Whisker—now Whisker is more a special friend."

"Whisker is a dog, I presume, sir?"

"No, a pony."

"Oh, a pony? Can't sleep on the bed. Can't wake you in the morning. Can't lick your hand, can't *miss* you. Never saw a pony that could do any of those things. Am I correct, sir?" said Pol.

"He's a special pony though," said Jemmy. "Very special." ·

"Don't doubt it, sir. As you are a special boy, sir."

Essence of dog

ARTIST UNKNOWN

Jemmy, whom nobody had ever called "special," was first embarrassed and then pleased.

"Yes," continued Pol. "A special boy. For what are you, my young friend? Are you a beast of the field? No. A bird of the air? Ah, a bird of the air, like our friend Grip there?"

Grip cawed quietly.

"No, sir," said Pol. "You are not a bird of the air. No. A fish of the sea or river? No, you are a human boy, my young friend. A special boy. A special boy needs a special friend. And it just so happens, sir, I have a special friend that needs a special boy. Come with me, sir. There," said Pol, pointing out to the back covert. "What is it, boy? What is it? Vegetable, sir? No, sir. Mineral, sir? No, sir. It is animal, sir. Dog, sir, essence of dog." Pol finished his litany and rubbed his hands.

"He's very big," said Jemmy. "Very big indeed."

"Watchdog, stable dog. Special dog," answered Pol.

And up loped Motley—a great, lumbering, enchanting Newfoundland, and sat down in front of Jemmy.

"Here's a boy for you, Motley. A special boy. Essence of boy. Now, go along, both of you. I'll have Grip back to Devonshire Terrace in a week."

"But you haven't told me," said Jemmy, hesitating, "you haven't told me why you call him Motley."

"Simple," said old Pol, "very simple. I think of the motley masquerade called human life. That's why I call him Motley. Simple."

"Oh, very," said Jemmy.

And Motley's great tail banged the ground in agreement.

16
Newfoundland Dog and Company

TRUE to his word, the bird fancier returned Grip to Devonshire Terrace. Cook and Topping were once more in residence. For that matter, so were the master and mistress. Children, of course. Ella naturally. It was a mystery, she said, where the summer had gone.

Old Pol let Grip flutter from his hands.

"I can't say I missed him," said Ella.

"Can't say, can't say," said old Pol with the very intonation of the parrots with whom he lived.

"He's always been a mystery," said Ella.

"You will pardon me, miss?"

Ella preened her own feathers at that.

"Yes, Mr. Pol?"

"It's the people who are the mystery." He rested his finger against his nose, and sniffed. "Essence of dog. I do believe I smell essence of dog."

"It's that Motley," said Cook, coming into the room as though she were young Queen Victoria deigning to give an audience.

Cook raised her regal, gastronomic nose. "Essence of dog, indeed. For which I believe, Mr. Pol, we are indebted to you. A great, black, thundering animal with the manners of—"

"A vagabond," supplied old Pol. "A drifter, a roamer, a pilgrim—"

"A pest," said Cook. "A great, hungry, monstrous pest. Why, if I would let him in here, I would have no need for a scullery maid. He cleans us, he does. Pots, pans, china, lobster. It's all the same to him. Shut that door behind you, Jemmy."

Jemmy shut it carefully. Then listened. Motley, who had learned that Cook would allow no scratching at the door, settled for a long sigh. Motley's lugubrious sighs could be heard for miles.

"No, he can't," said Cook.

"I know he can't," said Jemmy. "I know he can't come in the kitchen. Besides, Motley is smart, *he* knows he can't come in the kitchen."

"Gregarious," said old Pol, "convivial, most convivial dog I've ever known."

"Why did you give him to Jemmy then?" said Cook.

"Yes," said Ella, "it's a mystery as to why you should give away such a great dog."

"The essence of dog," said old Pol, greatly appreciating the cup of tea Ella had slopped before him.

"Excellent," said old Pol. "The essence of tea."

"Yes, why did you, Pol?" said Jemmy, eager to clarify his rights to such a magnificent animal.

Pol munched contentedly on the currant scone Cook had placed before him. Grip was clasped to his shoulder; and the two, the giant birdlike man and the small black raven, considered the scone before they considered Jemmy's question.

Old Pol picked up the scone and examined it on all sides.

"Currants. Grip here likes currants. Beautiful scone, if I may say so, Cook, shot through with the essence of currants."

He removed all the currants, one by one, and arranged them neatly in two piles.

"One for Grip. One for Pol. One for Pol. One for Grip."

When they had dispatched the currants, the crumpled scone seemed to confuse old Pol. Indeed, it had been a long time since he had sat in the same room with, yes, so many people. People

Dog fanciers were familiar sights in Dickens' London

DORÉ

made demands on poor Pol. People could not whistle. People could not sing with all nature in their throats. People could not crow. Old Pol shook his head in despair. That was the trouble. People were not birds.

"You see, sir," he said to Jemmy. "People are not animals of the field. Correct, sir? Nor fish of the water—"

Ella took this opportunity to turn on her heel and mutter to Cook.

"Mad."

"Don't interrupt a gentleman," said Cook severely.

From outside the door, Motley allowed a sigh to escape from the very depths of his being—a sigh of melancholy, a sigh that only a Newfoundland can make, a sigh of one hundred and fifty pounds of sorrow, a sigh of neglect, of nonappreciation. Then suddenly a quiet wail. At least Motley seemed to think it a quiet wail. But it gave Ella a terrible turn, it did. It was a mystery, said Ella, how Motley could sound like Mr. Mould, the cemetery man.

Old Pol, without even Cook intervening, went to the door, opened it, and gave Motley the piece of crumpled scone. Motley consumed it in one gulp. And then smiled.

"I told you," said Jemmy. "Cook, look for yourself. He smiles."

"Made me feel silly," Cook said later. The dog smiling on one side of the pantry door and Cook smiling on the other. That's how she happened to say, "Come in."

And Motley accepted the invitation.

"Essence of hospitality," said old Pol. "You asked me why you, essence of boy, Jemmy, should be the proud owner of such a magnificent dog. First, of course, every stable *needs* a dog."

Jemmy knew this was true. Even Mr. Dickens was delighted with the Newfoundland. It was *right* to have a dog.

"But you love him," said Jemmy.

"I do indeed," said old Pol.

And Motley thumped his tail so dramatically that the hanging pots gave off a faint music.

"Fear, sir," said old Pol.

"Fear?" said Jemmy. Old Pol didn't seem frightened of anything.

"Birds, sir."

"Birds?" said Jemmy. "Who can be afraid of birds?"

At this Ella sniffed. And Grip, who had been silent, let out a large "Pop."

Jemmy smiled at him. What a corking good bird he was.

"Powl," said Grip. "Powl." He jumped around happily.

"He's glad to be home," said Cook.

"Pol, Pol, Pol." Grip jumped and reeled with delight, and landed like a highly gifted circus performer on Motley's back. Motley took it stoically.

"You see, sir," said old Pol to Jemmy, "my birds frightened him. Birds in a group will gang up. Frightened Motley, they did. But Grip. No, indeed. Essence of dog and essence of bird should be an example to us all."

Guests

CRUIKSHANK

"Essence of friendship," said Pol, taking his leave. "And, madame"—he bowed to Cook—"you are welcome anytime to my humble abode."

Ella showed him out, and then began to sneeze. She sneezed and coughed and whimpered.

"What's the matter with her *now?*" said Cook.

"I'll take him out," said Jemmy. "I'll take them both out."

When Grip and Motley were safely stabled, Jemmy stuck his head in the kitchen again. "How's Ella?"

"I'm making her a vinegar plaster," said Cook. "A vinegar

plaster will cure anything."

"I know what's the matter with her," said Jemmy. "Simple. Essence of dog fur, essence of feathers—and worst of all—"

"Yes," said Cook sternly.

"Essence of Ella."

Cook threw a scone at him.

17
Let Nothing You Dismay

"HALLOA, old girl."

Cook looked down at the little imp. Grip had picked up that expression, perhaps from old Pol the bird fancier, who greeted all his birds—male and female alike—with that expression.

"Halloa, old girl."

Cook couldn't help smiling. Grip never used it to anyone else she noticed, and although it was ridiculous, yes ridiculous, to feel that a bird really noticed one, one did feel kind of privileged. Yes, that was the word, privileged. Grip had become a king in the kitchen. He had taken first place in the Dickens animal kingdom. And since that near-miss with the paint, this Christmas season all (except Ella) enjoyed him more.

"Feeling chipper, are you, Grip? None the worse for wear, are you? I wouldn't think that old bird fancier had such skill. Lives in a bird's nest, that man does. I wouldn't believe it if I didn't see it with my own eyes. Yes, a bird's nest."

"Pol," cried out Grip. "Pol, pol, polly, polly, part—" He had just noticed Ella coming in the kitchen.

"Don't try to be friends, Grip. I still think you had something to do with my comb."

"Old Pol said that was impossible. Grip was probably sick long before you missed your comb. Probably fell out of the window . . ."

"I saw a bird," said Ella stubbornly. "Constable believed me."

"I guess he did," Cook grumbled. "Over here often enough, warming himself on tea and crumpets."

"He's a gentleman."

"Well, that gentleman better stay out from underfoot with Christmas coming."

"A quiet one, I suspect," said Ella, hoping it would be. "The madam having a baby coming along, and the master all tied up in that book."

" 'Old Curiosity,' he calls it," said Cook, fixing her cap more firmly. "Old Curiosity has him all right. Up and out walking at all hours of the night."

"Pol," cried Grip. He appeared to understand that Ella's old distrust of him had returned. He made no effort to tease her, indeed, tried to prove to her that his visit with Pol, the bird fancier, had not only cured his frail bird body but made him an upstanding moral bird.

Ella felt she knew better. Constable Hunt said ravens were thieves, just like jackdaws.

"Constable said—" But Cook wouldn't let Ella continue.

"Pol," said Grip.

"Who's he talking about?" said Ella. "That awful bird fancier? I saw that house, Cook. Could you believe it?"

"I saw it myself," said Cook. "Gamecocks in the kitchen."

"Bantams in the cellar," shuddered Ella.

"Owls in his bedroom," said Jemmy, coming in suddenly. "Are you talking about old Pol? It's the truth, Cook. He takes me through the whole house now. Pheasants are all the way up in the garret. Birds twittering and chirping everywhere. And rabbits all over the staircase."

Cook sniffed. "Looks like a bird, anyway, that man. I've heard the neighbor cook say he's like a bird. Not a hawk or eagle, mind you, but a sparrow, yes, just like a sparrow. You know, the kind that builds in dark chimneys and inclines to human company."

"Halloa, old girl." Grip started jumping around.

"That's one that inclines to human company," Cook said, nodding toward Grip. "But I can't take you Christmas shopping."

Cook decided she would go down to Billingsgate market herself to choose the oysters and lobsters. That was always a treat for her.

"Halloa, old girl."

"Not now, Grip."

Yes, Billingsgate in the morning. A Cornish woman, she loved the feel of the sea that always overcame her at the Billingsgate fish market. Besides, only *she* really knew her fish.

"What are you thinking of, Cook?" asked Jemmy, surprised to see Cook so withdrawn into her world.

"Billingsgate."

"Billingsgate? That smelly old place?"

"It's got a nice smell to it, that market," said Cook fiercely. "A lot of people don't like it. But I think it's got a beautiful smell. It's got the smell of seaweed. Oh, it reminds you of the seashore. And then as you plunge deep into the market, you get the smell of the fish. You don't even have to take a look as to where they are. You can smell them if you've got a good nose on you. And most of us Cornish have that. Oh, you can smell welks, herring, sprats. You can see them in your mind's eye before you even get there. And at the end of the market you see the oyster boats. But always you'll hear the yelling and the bawling. 'Handsome cod! Best in the market. All alive. All alive-o. Come now. Come now. Hello, hello. Beautiful lobsters. Good and cheap. Fine caught crabs. All alive. All alive-o. Come, come. Skate. Had, had, had, haddock. All fresh and good. Come, you buyers. Come along. Come along. You're just in time for fine mussels. There's food for the belly and clothes for the back, but I sell food for the mind. Here's smelts. Here you are—fine finnan haddie.' "

Why, thought Jemmy, Cook was as good as a piece of theater.

Billingsgate Market as the fish come in

DORÉ

"That's good," said Jemmy. "That's very good. Give us some more."

"After Billingsgate," said Cook, noticing she had picked up an audience, "I'll get my vegetables. You can take me with Whisker, if you will, Jemmy—from Longacre to the Strand on one side and from Bow Street to Bedford on t'other. It's a picture, those vegetables, Jemmy. Cabbages that look like mountains. Cauliflowers as big as Piccadilly Circus . . ."

"Not quite, Cook," said Topping, scratching his red head and motioning Jemmy into the pantry.

"What's the matter with Cook?" asked Jemmy. "Cook looks as though she's about to cry."

"Homesick. Always is at Christmas," said Topping, holding one finger visibly beside his nose. "Seen it happen before. She'll forget about it as soon as she starts cooking."

"I feel it myself," said Jemmy.

"Just stay out from underfoot, Grip. Christmas is acoming," said Cook.

And as she did every year, she began to compose in her head the litany of Christmas dinner:

The fine turkey that the master's printers sent every year, two fat geese, two substantial chickens. Sausages, pies, puddings, the pheasants from Mr. Maclise (he had plenty, he said, because the Queen had supplied his table) . . . and, let us see, oysters, of course, lobster, perhaps only a shilling apiece.

"Mr. Dickens says . . ."

"Mr. Dickens says what?" said Cook, pulling herself together.

"He said, everybody should go home for Christmas."

"Pretend, anyway, I guess he means," said Jemmy.

"Busy, busy. Let's get busy," said Cook.

Yes, she must have oranges and lemons, plump raisins, and almonds, white as the snow that had just begun to fall, and French plums, and, and, and . . . and Christmas was coming. How Mr. Dickens did love Christmas!

18
A Very Queer Character

"GRIP, you look very ruffled today. Have you been keeping bad company?"

Grip did not answer Dickens. He turned his back, waited a while, and let out a long "Pop."

Birds were not too discriminating, thought Dickens, about their company. He had noticed that many a scoundrel kept birds. But so, for that matter, did the Queen. Birds, as did most pets, took on some of the qualities of their owners.

Who had been the "unknown admirer" who had wished Grip on Dickens? What sort of a person would befriend Grip? If one were to write a story . . .

Put a bird in jail. Now what made him think of that? Dickens knew in the story that he had just started to write *Barnaby Rudge*, that not only Barnaby, the poor retarded boy, but his pet, Grip, would eventually be in jail. But all of that was ahead. Stories developed. Dickens loved to publish everything in serial form; it was exciting to see what emerged in the next chapter of any book or any story. He was fascinated by the way Grip was becoming a character, and without the presence of this bird in the house, he would have missed a great deal.

Grip had learned much since he had arrived. His own limited vocabulary had been enlarged, but now, as Dickens watched Grip, he often seemed to be trying out phrases and sentences. What was he doing now? "Pop, pop, pop"—his usual popping

Grip as he appears in "Barnaby Rudge"

PHIZ

sound. What a corking good bird he was. "Pop, pop, pop. Powl," said Grip. "Powl," and jumped around in excitement the way all of us do if, after a terrible problem, we have found a solution. "Powl, powl, powl." And Grip jumped and reeled with delight. "Powl, powl, powl. Polly, Polly, Polly."

Dickens sat there and laughed. The raven was fabulous entertainment. "Polly, Polly what?" said Dickens.

"Pah, pah, pah," said Grip. And that was that for the day.

It was time, thought Dickens, for Grip to be immortalized in print and picture. Yes, it was very much time for Grip to make his way into the world.

"How would you like to have your picture drawn, Grip?"

Grip answered nothing to that. He was still trying out "Pol, Pol, Pol, Polly."

"Your picture, Grip," said Dickens. "How would you like your picture drawn?"

Suddenly Grip looked directly at him and gave a crow with

such duration as a cock might. He considered what Dickens had said and then suddenly came out with his newest expression. "Never say die," said Grip. "Never say die."

He repeated it a great many times and flapped his wings for emphasis. And then, because it was a cold day, he moved closer to the fire. He perched on one leg, prepared to doze in the grateful warmth. A profound silence followed as he tried to recall his new accomplishment. Grip tried the words again, "Polly, Polly, Polly put, Polly put, Polly put." And Dickens picked up pen and paper and began to write to a prospective illustrator for *Barnaby Rudge:*

> Devonshire Terrace
> Thursday Night
> January 28, 1941

My dear George,

I sent to Chapman and Hall yesterday morning, about the second subject of No. 2 of *Barnaby* . . .

I want to know whether you *feel* Ravens in general, and would fancy Barnaby's raven in particular. Barnaby being an idiot, my notion is to have him always in company with a pet raven who is immeasurably more knowing than himself. To this end, I have been studying my bird, and think I could make a very queer character of him. Should you like the subject when this raven makes his first appearance?

> Faithfully Always
> Charles Dickens

19
Surprise!

"I'LL HELP you write," said young Charley to his father. "See, I'll help you," and the Living Wonder picked up a pen from Dickens' desk and settled himself on the floor with a stack of paper.

Dickens observed him carefully. New ideas about infant education were much in the air.

Writing was a trying business to Charley. He seemed to have no natural power over a pen. First he bespattered himself with a rain of ink, then he stared at the pen. It had become perversely animated. The pen seemed to go wrong and crooked, and to stop and splash and sidle into corners in a fashion as contrary as the pony Whisker.

It was very odd to see what old letters Charley's young hand had made. His little hand was so round and plump; his letters in contrast were wrinkled, shriveled, and tottering. Yet, the Living Wonder was uncommonly expert at many things.

"Here," said Charley.

He handed his father some examples of his work.

"Well, Charley," said Dickens, looking at the letter O that Charley had given him. "Well, Charley."

Dickens studied the O. Sometimes it was squared, sometimes it was triangular, sometimes it was pear-shaped. This time it had collapsed.

"Well, Charley. We are improving."

Severe weather

ARTIST UNKNOWN

"Then, we'll go out," said Charley.

"Out, out, out into February," said Dickens.

Once outside, Charley ran ahead to talk to the gardener.

"Severe weather," said Charley, racing back to his father. "That's what the gardener says. He's found something, he says."

"Oh, and what would that be?" said Dickens. "A polar bear skating?"

"No, Papa. No, Papa."

"A muffin-man blown over the wall by the wind?"

"No, no, no, Papa."

"A veal pie smoking in the snow?"

"No, no. A comb, a comb, a comb. And a nest."

"Aha," said Dickens. "Show me this February wonder."

"A rook's nest, sir," said the gardener. "And smack in it is Ella's comb. Always knew Grip didn't take it. Grip couldn't fly up that high."

"Good Grip," said Charley.

"Excellent Grip," said Dickens. "I'll relieve you of that comb, please; I have plans for it."

"What plans?" said Charley, skipping along in the snow. "Won't we give the comb to Ella?"

"Of course," said Dickens. "But not immediately."

"A surprise?"

"Yes, a surprise."

Motley, at that point, came out of the stable door. He looked for a minute as though he were a black winter thundercloud, deliberately deciding where he would attack. Then he gathered speed, growing more exuberant and joyous as he moved, his great haunches churning, churning as though they were powered by steam—a locomotive of a dog. Obviously he aimed to pull into the station—his place beside Dickens and the Living Wonder in their turn around the garden. But Motley, as he often did, misjudged his strength. He came to a stop with such force, he toppled Charley and the world's greatest living author into a snowbank.

"Speaking of surprises . . .," said Dickens, struggling to his feet and pulling Charley up as well.

"Woof," barked Motley. "Bowwow, yeugh, yeugh."

This loud declaration of love and affection summoned everyone—gardener, Topping, Jemmy, and even Cook, armed, in case of battle, with a large fry pan, and for good measure, a steaming teakettle.

"I think," said Dickens, addressing one and all, "in the matter of affections, Motley was pitched neck and crop into the world to play leapfrog with its troubles. Cook, please, tea upstairs. A collation—and, if you please, a word with you, please. I am planning a party."

20
Valentine Magic

"A PARTY," sniffed Ella. "Work, that's what it is."

"Work," said Cook. "Are you implying that it's your work, Ella?"

"And a St. Valentine's party at that!" At which point, Ella distorted her face to give prominence to the lovely tear that balanced on the end of her nose. She thought about heaving her shoulders with suffering, but that would dislodge the iridescent drop of water.

Everyone sat around the table entranced. Cook covered her mouth, holding herself in like a Christmas pudding that would burst its binding. Topping had a saucer of tea halfway to his mouth. Jemmy had tea in his mouth, and dared not swallow. The three of them waited for the tear to drop. Ella disappointed all of them. Her long tongue darted out like a lizard's, licked the tear up, and it was gone.

When the drama had subsided, Topping, as much an actor as his master, said quietly, "Letter just come."

"My brother, I guess," said Cook. Brother was always complaining, so she made no further effort.

"Delivered by a royal footman?" said Jemmy. No letter ever came for him.

"Delivered by Constable Hunt," said Topping. "Letter smells."

"Smells?" said Cook.

A St. Valentine's party

LEECH

Topping picked up the pink envelope. "Yes, smells."

"Give me that," said Ella. "It's mine; I know it's mine. I was crying because I hadn't heard from him."

Ella tore it from Topping's hand and disappeared.

"Valentine," said Topping, grinning. "How's the master's dinner coming? He's going to do magic."

Topping took his master very much as he found him. He was not impressed by Dickens the celebrity, or Dickens the writer, or Dickens the rich man. But Dickens the magician delighted him. "Demon fingers, he's got. I'll say that for him. Demon fingers."

"Started as a child," said Cook. "Once he came down here and made a piece of Sally Lunn disappear before my eyes."

"Easy, if he ate it," said Jemmy.

"Magic, boy. He did it by magic."

Dickens' demon fingers, were, said Jane Carlyle, as nimble as birds that night. First, he had distributed a delightful program that read:

The Leaping Cards Wonder

Two Cards being drawn from the Pack by two of the company, and placed, with the pack, in the Necromancer's box, will leap forth at the command of any lady of not less than eight, or more than eighty, years of age.

This wonder is the result of nine years' seclusion in the mines of Russia.

The Pyramid Wonder

A shilling being lent to the Necromancer by any gentleman of not less than twelve months, or more than one hundred years, of age, and carefully marked by the said gentleman, will disappear from within a brazen box at the word of command, and pass through the hearts of an infinity of boxes, which will afterwards build themselves into pyramids and sink into a small mahogany box, at the Necromancer's bidding.

Five thousand guineas were paid for the acquisition of this wonder, to a Chinese Mandarin, who died of grief immediately after parting with the secret.

THE CONFLAGRATION WONDER

A Card being drawn from the Pack by any lady, not under a direct and positive promise of marriage, will be immediately named by the Necromancer, destroyed by fire, and reproduced from its own ashes.

An annuity of one thousand pounds has been offered to the Necromancer by the Directors of the Sun Fire Office for the secret of this wonder—and refused!!!

THE LOAF OF BREAD WONDER

The watch of any truly prepossessing lady, of any age, single or married, being locked by the Necromancer in a strong box, will fly at the word of command from within that box into the heart of an ordinary half-quartern loaf, whence it shall be cut out in the presence of the whole company, whose cries of astonishment will be audible at a distance of some miles.

Ten years in the Plains of Tartary were devoted to the study of this wonder.

THE TRAVELLING DOLL WONDER

The travelling doll is composed of solid wood throughout, but, by putting on a travelling dress of the simplest construction, becomes invisible, performs enormous journeys in half a minute, and passes from visibility to invisibility with an expedition so astonishing that no eye can follow its transformations.

The Necromancer's attendant usually faints on beholding this wonder, and is only to be revived by the administration of brandy and water.

A Present for Charles Dickens

THE PUDDING WONDER

The company having agreed among themselves to offer to the Necromancer, by way of loan, the hat of any gentleman whose head has arrived at maturity of size, the Necromancer, without removing that hat for an instant from before the eyes of the delighted company, will light a fire in it, make a plum-pudding in his magic saucepan, boil it over the said fire, produce it in two minutes, thoroughly done, cut it, and dispense it in portions to the whole company, for their consumption then and there; returning the hat at last, wholly uninjured by fire, to its lawful owner.

The extreme liberality of this wonder awakening the jealousy of the beneficent Austrian Government, when exhibited in Milan, the Necromancer had the honour to be seized, and confined for five years in the fortress of that city.

At the last trick, Dickens called for everyone from downstairs. There in front of all, he magically made the pudding, cut it up, and extracted . . . *one silver comb!*

"Well," Ella gasped, and said it was a mystery. She was delighted to have her comb back, however strange its reappearance.

But Cook was somewhat disappointed. She didn't know quite what Dickens did or how he did it, but she, for one, had followed the master's instruction and baked the comb in the pudding.

Strange doings, and stranger yet when Ella went to the stable to apologize to Grip for her accusations that he had stolen her comb.

"Only fitting," said Jemmy.

But Grip took no interest. No interest at all. It was at that point, Ella said later, that she had a Foreboding Feeling. But alas, no one took further notice of Ella's feelings. They had had "quite sufficient," as Cook said, "for the day."

21
The Letter with an Enormous Black Seal

"IT WAS a mystery. Dear Grip dead," Ella moaned and howled. Cook was so taken that she could not subdue her. Jemmy was speechless. He had been unable to find Pol. Topping muttered, "Good riddance" (quite under his breath). Mrs. Dickens was too busy with a brand-new baby to consider the news. Young Charley had been so smothered by the affection of Motley, the Newfoundland hurricane, that the small bird had almost been forgotten.

Dickens did as he often did, put the tragedy down on paper.

Devonshire Terrace.
Friday Evening
March The Twelfth 1841

My dear Maclise,
You will be greatly shocked and grieved to hear that the Raven is no more.

He expired to-day at a few minutes after Twelve o'Clock at noon. He had been ailing (as I told you t'other night) for a few days, but we anticipated no serious result, conjecturing that a portion of the white paint he swallowed last summer might be lingering about his vitals without having any serious effect upon his constitution. Yesterday afternoon he was taken so much worse that I sent an express for the medical gentleman (Mr. Herring) who promptly attended and administered a powerful dose of castor oil. Under the influence of this medicine, he recovered so far as to be able at 8 o'Clock P.M. to bite Topping. His night was peaceful. This morning at daybreak he appeared better; received (agreeably to the doctor's directions) another dose of castor oil; and partook plentifully of some warm gruel, the flavor of which he appeared to relish. Towards 11 o'Clock he was so much worse that it was found necessary to muffle the stable knocker. At half past, or thereabouts, he was heard talking to himself about the horse and Topping's family, and to add some incoherent expressions which are supposed to have been either a foreboding of his

Memorial for Grip drawn by Daniel Maclise

approaching dissolution, or some wishes relative to the disposal of his little property—consisting chiefly of halfpence which he had buried in different parts of the garden. On the clock striking twelve he appeared slightly agitated, but he soon recovered, walked twice or thrice along the coach-house, stopped to bark, staggered, exclaimed "Halloa, old girl!" (his favorite expression) and died.

He behaved throughout with a decent fortitude, equanimity, and self-possession, which cannot be too much admired. I deeply regret that being in ignorance of his danger I did not attend to receive his last instructions. Something remarkable about his eyes occasioned Topping to run for the doctor at Twelve. When they returned together our friend was gone. It was the medical gentleman who informed me of his decease. He did it with great caution and delicacy, preparing me by the remark that "a jolly queer start had taken place," but the shock was very great notwithstanding.

I am not wholly free from suspicions of poison—a malicious butcher has been heard to say that he would "do" for him—his plea was that he would not be molested in taking orders down the Mews, by any bird that wore a tail. Other persons have also been heard to threaten—among others, Charles Knight who has just started a weekly publication, price fourpence, Barnaby being, as you know, Threepence. I have directed a post mortem examination, and the body has been removed to Mr. Herring's school of Anatomy for that purpose.

I could wish, if you can take the trouble, that you could enclose this to Forster when you have read it. I cannot discharge the painful task of communication more than once. Were they Ravens who took Manna to somebody in the wilderness? At times I hope they were, and at others I fear they were not, or they would certainly have stolen it by the way. In profound sorrow, I am ever Your bereaved friend, C. D.

Kate is as well as can be expected, but terribly low as you may suppose. The children seem rather glad of it. He bit their ankles. But that was play.

Dickens sealed it with an enormous black seal.

22
"I've Seen a Ghost!"

"I'M COMING. I'm coming," cried Ella, making for the front door. "It's a mystery why people bang, bang, bang on the door knocker. One knock is enough. Knock you out of peace and quiet."

"Yes." Ella enjoyed looking down on people. It was a young wretch, it was. No bigger than Jemmy. With a box.

"Tradesman's door. Downstairs."

She banged the door. It didn't shut properly, so she banged it again. At the third bang, it closed to her satisfaction. She smiled smugly and looked straight ahead. She had been out for a walk with Constable Hunt last night and felt fuzzy in the head, like a caterpillar. And her hair. Her hair. The constable had brought up the mystery of her comb. That Grip! He was such a subject of conversation. More than ever, now that he was dead. She was miserable about accusing the bird of stealing her comb. He hadn't. But if he could have, he would have. After all, he was a . . . "Rascal."

With that very word on her lips, she ran into—the master. "Oh, sir."

"Surely, I'm not the rascal," said Dickens.

"I was thinking of Grip, sir."

"So was I," said Dickens. "And the commotion at the door?"

"Tradesman with a box," said Ella, blushing, wringing her hands, twisting her hair, and straightening her apron, and all at once. At sixes and sevens she was this morning.

"A box," said Dickens thoughtfully. "Boxes are the joys of my life. See what's in it, Ella. Come back and tell me."

"It's a mystery," wailed Ella, clumping down the stairs. "Boxes are boxes. Why should people love boxes? Stupid things, boxes. Hard to open."

"Is that you muttering?" called Cook, who came out of her private buttery, rubbing her floury hands on her morning apron. She had a lilac ribbon running through her starched cap, and, thought Jemmy, who had admired the cap, a starched look on her face. She had had that look on her face ever since Grip died. So starched it was, her face, that it looked like a great dry biscuit. One touch, and it would crumble.

She hadn't cried when Grip died. Just went into her room, came out with cornstarch on her face, walking stiff and strange-like. Never laughed. Never even smiled.

Jemmy didn't understand it. He had cried. Came on him very unexpected. He had buried his head in Whisker's mane—the sharp hair scratched his eyes, and suddenly he was crying, snorting, sniffing, sneezing. Felt a lot better, too.

Not Cook.

"There's a box here, Jemmy. Open it." Cook was all orders now. No smiles. No fancy collations. Gave you cold tea and cold looks.

"Easy enough to open," said Jemmy, sliding the stick that closed the great wicker box.

"Master wants to know what's in it," said Ella.

"What did you close it again for," said Cook. "Get off it, Jemmy. What are you getting on it for?"

"Surprised," said Jemmy. "Just surprised." He said nothing more. He looked at Cook and Ella. Cook and Ella looked at him.

"Get off, I said," said Cook. "Get off and get to the stables. That's where the dumb animals live. Get!" And she went for a broom. Jemmy scuttled through the door, grabbed Motley by the

collar, and raced for the stables. Once there, he knelt, pulled
Motley to him, and the dog, as was his custom, put his ear to
Jemmy's mouth to hear his secret.

"A ghost," whispered Jemmy.

"A ghost." Motley took the words and examined them as he
would a bone. Then all his hair stood on end as though he were
some spectral dog himself.

It was in that frozen tableau that Topping found them.

"I've seen a ghost," said Jemmy.

"You'll see the inside of cleaning out a stable," said Topping,
pretending to give him a cuff. Then Topping scratched his early
morning beard and said, "A ghost, Jemmy?"

"Yes," said Jemmy. "A ghost."

In the meantime, Ella and Cook were busy exchanging
kitchen glances. I'll look if you'll look. You do it. No, you do it.
Let it stay. No, open it. Finally both moved toward the box.

Ella pulled out the stick.

Cook opened it.

Both looked in.

"A mystery," screamed Ella. "A ghost. A ghost." She
straightened up, looked toward the heavens, and fainted. A nice,
neat, squared faint. Her feet up like little flags.

Cook smiled.

A giant raven waited for the excitement to calm down. Then
skipped out of the box, gave his coat a shake as though it needed a
good freshening up. He looked, as Cook said later, with proper
disgust at Ella, walked around to her pointed feet, stepped up
upon them. Waited for her to open her eyes, caught her startled
look, opened that great beak, and said, "Home."

And so it was that Grip II set up housekeeping at Devonshire
Terrace.

About This Story

CHARLES DICKENS, a great lover of animals, was the "proud possessor" of two ravens.

The first, he said, "was in the bloom of his youth, when he was discovered in a modest retirement in London, by a friend of mine, and given to me. He had, from the first, as Sir Hugh Evans says of Anne Page, 'good gifts' which he improved by study and attention in a most exemplary manner. He slept in a stable—

generally on horseback—and so terrified a Newfoundland dog by his preternatural sagacity, that he has been known, by the mere superiority of his genius, to walk off unmolested with the dog's dinner, from before his face. He was rapidly rising in acquirements and virtues, when, in an evil hour, his stable was newly painted. He observed the workmen closely, so that they were careful of the paint, and immediately burned to possess it. On their going to dinner, he ate up all they had left behind, consisting of a pound or two of white lead; and this youthful indiscretion terminated in death."

I found this description of Grip irresistible, and it is the basis of my story, filled in like an old holiday pudding with currants and citron of the imagination as well as the flavors of old diaries, letters, and other contemporary chronicles.

Ravens are capable of speech, but the liberties I take with Grip, his huge talent for speech, follow those used by Dickens himself when he depicted Grip in *Barnaby Rudge*.

I am grateful to many for contributing to this amusement. I would like to thank the late Dr. Robert Cushman Murphy, curator emeritus of the American Museum of Natural History, who encouraged my early interest in corvine capers; Dr. David Parker, curator of the Dickens House Museum, London, England, who shares my interest in Dickens' appreciation of animals; and Mr. Howell Heaney, librarian emeritus of the Rare Book Room of The Free Library of Philadelphia, who not only read the manuscript but who was the guardian of Grip himself, now stuffed but ever triumphant in the library.

Miss Jane Kendall searched for many books for me in both England and the United States. My daughter, Shivaun Manley, and my nieces Carol Lewis and Sara Lewis all did research in England, which was valuable. Ms. Susan Andews and Ms. Karen Lorenz also helped. My own British friends are so many and so dear that I take this opportunity to thank all of them for their hospitality and good conversation.

Finally, I am deeply appreciative of those who prepared this manuscript for the press, particularly Betty Shalders, Susan Belcher, my sister, Gogo Lewis, and my husband, Robert, who felt the ghost of Grip nipping at his ankles on more than one occasion.

Grip I was preserved by a taxidermist and treasured by Dickens. He is now among friends in the Rare Book Room of The Free Library of Philadelphia. "The Graphic" published this picture of the "late Mr. Charles Dickens' raven" in October 1870

ARTIST UNKNOWN

About the Illustrations

ALL illustrations are by artists contemporary with Dickens.

GEORGE CRUIKSHANK (1792–1879) was the original illustrator of *Oliver Twist* and other Dickens novels. See pp. 27, 83.

PAUL GUSTAVE DORÉ (1833–1883) was a French illustrator who followed Dickens in portraying London scenes. The frontispiece is from his collection entitled *London*. For other engravings, see pp. 51, 61, 66, 75, 81, 89.

JOHN LEECH (1817–1864) was an English caricaturist and illustrator of several of Dickens' works. See p. 99.

DANIEL MACLISE (1806–1870) was an Irish historical painter who designed illustrations for some of Dickens' Christmas books. See pp. 7, 104.

PHIZ was Hablot Knight Browne (1815–1882), a major illustrator chosen by Dickens for his books. See pp. 20, 22, 92.

"CHRISTMAS CHATTERBOX" was one of the many holiday annuals, collections of stories, poems, and amusements issued by children's magazines, which are still numerous and popular today in England. See p. 49.

The drawings of members of the crow family (p. 3) are from *The Animal Kingdom*, selected by Reverend W. Bingley, A. M. Hubbard Brothers, nineteenth century.

In selecting and reproducing the engravings from old books,

magazines, and papers, I have had the help of my sister, Gogo Lewis, who supervised their preparation for publication. I would also like to thank Barbara-Ann Colgan, Dorothy Rodriguez, and Edward Mitchell.

About the Author

SEON MANLEY is a longtime historian of the supernatural story and a frequent speaker, reviewer, and writer on a wide variety of topics. She is well known in the literary world both as an author and as an editor. She was born in Connecticut and attended Wellesley College. Mrs. Manley makes her home in Greenwich, Connecticut.

copy 1 HQ

J   Manley, Seon
Manley   Present for Charles
        Dickens.

CHESAPEAKE PUBLIC LIBRARY

Chesapeake, Virginia

RULES

1. Books may be kept two weeks and may renewed once for the same period.

2. A fine will be charged on each book which is not returned according to the above rule. No book will be issued to any person incurring such a fine until it has been paid.

3. All injuries to books beyond reasonable wear and all losses shall be made good to the satisfaction of the Librarian.

4. Each borrower is held responsible for all books drawn on his card and for all fines accruing on the same.